GRACE AND GRIT

KIM SMART

This book is dedicated to all those friends who have shared some element of life's journey with me, family with whom I have ridden the ups and downs, and others who have shared their quest to feel, explore, and overcome life's challenges to bring their light into the world. Your light is treasured!

1

———————

*A*ngela pushed through the door of her Manhattan apartment, pulled the hospital scrubs off and tossed them into the washer on the way to the shower. Turning up the volume on the radio app, she sang along as the day's work slid off her tired body and circled the drain. For months the hospital had been short-staffed with a high patient load. She loved being a nurse, and the emergency room was her haven, but she was exhausted. The trip to Bella's couldn't have come at a better time. Any guilt felt for leaving coworkers, and there was some, would have to fall away into the ethers somewhere over Illinois. Angela didn't have the energy to even will it away right now.

"Hey Joel, this is Angela in apartment 13B." She paused for a second to catch her breath and calm the frenzied feeling. "Oh, of course you can tell who it is, sorry. I'm running late but have an Uber coming by. Can you please let the driver in a blue Toyota Camry know I'll be right out?"

Angela barely listened to the concierge-slash-doorman's

response as she reached down to zip the new Freebird leather boots and tugged the belt on the new Tanya Taylor sundress into place. Passing by the mirror, she paused to admire the new designer travel clothes. Yes, she would make the transition to country girl just fine. She smiled, checked her bright white teeth for lipstick smears, and snatched the new straw cowgirl hat from the Nordstrom shopping bag.

Before zipping the designer suitcase, Angela peered and patted through its contents one last time to ensure that Marco's present got packed. She missed the boy terribly, but knew he was thriving on the ranch, with his own horse, new friends at school, and now a new baby sister. The Oculus she got him was all the rage, according to her co-workers, and when the cute young store clerk walked her through the demo, she knew it was just the right gift for a curious boy. She hoped he didn't already have one.

A FEW MINUTES LATER, dragging the luggage behind, Angela strutted across the marble lobby and blew a kiss to Joel. "I'll be back in two weeks. Keep an eye on things for me and I'll bring you a souvenir."

"I certainly will, Miss Angela. Enjoy your trip and give Miss Bella and Master Marco a big squeeze from Uncle Joel."

In some circles, referring to himself as Uncle Joel would come across as creepy, but Angela knew that Joel was a harmless widower with children and grandchildren of his own. He had conducted the business of the apartment building lobby for over thirty-five years and was a consummate professional. Angela often accessed his years of experience and wisdom when she needed personal advice, especially now that Bella was a million miles away.

A stranger to no one, Angela's full day of travel, including a layover in Minneapolis, flew by. There were no direct flights between LaGuardia and Rapid City. "A sure sign that you're headed to the middle of nowhere," she had told a flight attendant when making this same journey for the first time, after her best friend Bella took a job on a ranch in the Badlands of South Dakota. After that flight, Angela watched in amazement as the same flight attendant slid into the passenger side of a raised four-wheel-drive pickup and kissed the driver. She chastised herself for her careless words. *"Sometimes, Angela, you really stick your foot in it."*

Angela didn't mind the flight into Rapid City. She had made it a few times since Bella fell in love with her Badlands rancher and left big-city life behind for good. Angela tucked the Brighton bag, a bridesmaid's gift from Bella, under the seat in front of her and gazed out the window. Fence lines, neatly drawn in the green countryside below, penned in cattle and kept the I-90 tourists out.

As they prepared to land, the kind woman in the middle seat smiled. "Thanks for chatting with me, Angela. It helped pass the time. I just know you and your friends will have a great time at the town celebration and christening. I bet they are very excited to see you, too." She reminded Angela of a music teacher she once had, filled with sunny warmth and a today-is-a-beautiful-day attitude.

"Thank you, Sue, and thanks for giving me your business card. I will be sure to share it with Bella and Steve. Don't be surprised if they invite you out to entertain sometime. I know they like having South Dakota talent for guests and the townsfolk to come out and enjoy."

"Their dude ranch sounds truly spectacular. I'll chat with my honey and maybe we'll just do a getaway weekend sometime. Between calving, planting, and harvesting, half our year is filled up, but by hunting season, maybe we can manage to get away, although that's when I start looking for gigs to play in the warmer parts of the country."

"I do hope you are able to get out to the ranch. There's a bit of magic there between their incredible hospitality, Steve's knowledge of the area, and Bella's scrumptious cooking. For you and your husband, being ranchers yourselves, that won't really be exceptional, but perched on the edge of the Badlands, with its history and good vibe, now that's where it's all happening." Angela started to feel like an ad. "Their son, Marco, is really awesome, too. I can't wait to see him. We were best buddies when we lived together in Manhattan."

"And that new baby! Can I see her picture again?" The youthful grandmother, singer, and rancher loved babies and had shared photos and action videos of her thirteen grandbabies.

Angela happily obliged. She pulled out her phone and opened the latest series of photos of Annie. She zoomed in on Marco holding his newborn sister. "This is my favorite."

"He looks like a wonderful big brother."

"He is. On the phone last night, he was telling me about the christening gown and the special brunch we will be having after church next weekend. He even picked out a new bolo tie to go with his best dress shirt. That boy!"

The plane bounced suddenly as the tires hit the runway. Angela sent a message to let Bella know they had landed, although she was sure she would be standing inside the terminal watching.

"Sue, it has been an absolute pleasure. Please excuse me as I move as quickly as I can to hug those babies."

"You enjoy, Angela! Hope to see you again one day."

Bella searched the deplaning passengers for her friend with the flaming red hair and long legs. She caught a glimpse of the ginger curls falling below a straw hat and raised her hand, waving and shouting to get Angela's attention.

"Oh, my, Marco, look at how much you've grown!" Angela dropped her Brighton bag and swept the boy into her arms. Marco went willingly into the beautiful friend's arms, letting his feet fly in the air as Angela twirled him around. "You're up to my…you're just so tall now!"

Angela looked to her dearest friend in the world and pushed her bottom lip out. "He's getting so big, momma."

"Don't I know it. We can hardly keep him in clothes. Thank goodness it's summertime and he can wear cut-offs." Bella reached one arm out to her friend while cradling the baby in the other. "Come here and give me some love."

Angela hugged the much shorter Bella, taking care not to crush the baby, then bent over the sleeping little bundle. "Oh, my gawd, she is gorgeous, aren't you baby girl?" Angela gently rubbed the little girl's tiny hands. "Where's Steve?"

"He dropped us off and parked the truck. He'll meet us down in baggage claim."

"Come on Auntie Angie, I'll show you where to go." Marco put his hand in hers and pulled her toward the escalator.

"There's Dad!" As they headed down, Marco pointed to the man Angela had come to love as a brother. He was the perfect match for her precious friend and had become more of a father to Marco than his own father ever was.

"Steve! It's so great to see you and to meet your beautiful daughter." Angela embraced Steve while Marco headed toward the conveyor belt.

"Is it the pink bag again, Auntie Angie?"

"Yep, but I had better help you. It's pretty heavy." Angela elbowed Steve, nodded toward Bella and Annie coming down the escalator, and swiftly moved across the baggage claim area to help Marco.

"On the count of three, let's grab it and lift it off. One, two, three..." She let Marco do the heavy lifting. He had become strong with all his ranch chores. "Well done, kind sir. Well done! Do you want to roll it for me?"

"Yes, ma'am, I do."

2

———

Angela was happy to be sandwiched between the children in the back seat of the pickup. Marco, with his heart-melting grin, excitedly caught Angela up on his days at the swimming pool, time with Steve's parents, the trail rides with Steve, and helping Steve's mom at the dude ranch café when Bella had the baby. "You should have seen me, Angie. I had an apron on and even poured the wine one night."

"Oh, honey, we really shouldn't talk about that part. Nana didn't know that it was not right for you to be serving guests the wine, but your dad and I are so grateful for your help."

Angela snickered as she looked at the blushing Bella.

"Of course he told that story at coffee one day with grandpa when the sheriff was there. The guys all had a good laugh, but the next time Steve saw Sheriff Klingdale, he encouraged us not to do that again. We never would have, and he knew that."

Looking to the right, Angela locked eyes with Annie, who was now awake. She had dark hair and petite features like her mom. "What does your mom think of the baby, Steve?"

"Oh, you'll see. She's in heaven! She's loved Marco since the day he arrived by surprise at the ranch, and she loves his little sister just as much. She's been great to help out this past month, especially those first two weeks that we convinced Bella to stay away from the dude ranch."

"Only two weeks off, Bella!?"

"Believe me, we tried to get her to take more time off, but she just wouldn't have it." Steve reported.

"That's right," Bella defended herself. "I love what we do there, and you know me. I'm not one to just sit around."

"Well, that's true enough." As they approached town, Angela looked out across to the westbound lanes of I-90. "I am always amazed at the traffic around here. It's such a small town, but it's as busy as the turnpike in the summertime."

"I would say not quite, but you are right that there is a lot of traffic. That's what makes the businesses so good around here."

"I'm sure it doesn't hurt the dude ranch either, does it?"

Steve loved their life on the ranch and running the dude ranch. Originally his late wife's dream, Steve and Bella worked together to create an incredible experience and maintain a family atmosphere by being the primary contacts with ranch guests. They had some help in the summer, from local workers at the greenhouse and housekeepers for cabins. "We are staying really busy and having a lot of fun. Just last week we had people from nine different countries as guests. You should have heard some of the campfire stories. These people came from all walks of life and did some incredible things."

"Dad, remember that guy who said he was a prince from some country? He was a cool dude, but he wasn't very good with Sassy, and she's such a good horse."

"Wow, that sounds like an interesting story. I can't wait to hear the rest of it."

They reached the intersection separating their destination in the country from the small tourist town. A large banner hung on the overpass: BUFFALO RIDGE 110TH ANNIVERSARY CELEBRATION JULY 9-11. Having lived in the city all her life, Angela was unfamiliar with small-town life, except what Bella shared. "You know, I've never been here for the town celebration. What kinds of things happen there?"

Steve glanced at Angela in the rearview mirror. "You're going to love it. Trust me."

"Yeah, Auntie, it's a blast. There's so much fun stuff. I did mutton busting last year and found money in the haystack. This year there will be a bouncy house. Oh, and there's a dance. You would probably like that."

"A dance? Really? Would you be my date, Marco?"

Marco wrinkled up his nose. "I don't want to date, but I'll go with you. My friend Joey's uncle plays the guitar in the band."

"Is that right. Then we need to at least go see if Joey's uncle is any good. Deal?"

"Deal, but can we get ice cream first?"

"Of course. Anything for you, my love." Angela pinched Marco's cheek as he turned five shades of crimson.

A FEW MINUTES later they turned off the main road and drove along the wall of the Badlands. The mountains, buttes, and mounds of the Badlands showed off their layered colors in the sunlight. Yellow, red, pink, and buff rows paralleled the horizon with hoodoos rising high above toward the bright blue sky. Several miles into the Badlands, Angela spotted the sign for the dude ranch. "Hey, look at that! There's a dude ranch around here."

"Of course, silly. We're headed home." Marco giggled as he elbowed his beloved Angela.

Baby Annie started to fuss just as their home came into view.

"Just in time. She's ready to eat and I'm ready to have her eat." Bella held one hand to her full chest. Annie was the best baby ever, and they had gotten into a routine already in their first month together. "Let me just go take care of her and then we will start serving dinner. Steve, will you help Angela get her bag into the spare room in the house while I take care of Annie? We can meet up in about a half-hour in the café."

Steve leaned in and kissed his wife. He loved her more each day and his heart swelled with the joy Annie brought to the whole family. "Of course. I see Mom's truck down at the café. I'll check in with her and see where things are. Angela, I'll show you to your room and you are free to stay at the house, come down to the café, or wander wherever. I would suggest, however, that you don't miss the campfire this evening. One of the local women is bringing her guitar out and she's got a great voice and some powerful music."

"Besides that, tonight is a full moon. What more could a city girl ask for on her first night back in the country?" Bella smiled at her friend. "But, can I suggest you wear sneakers or Tevas? You never know when you might find a snake hole around here."

"You and your snake stories! I'm not falling for those again. But, just in case there's a prairie dog hole, I will put on my hiking sandals, thank you very much."

TRUE TO STEVE'S WORDS, the evening campfire was a blast. Angela showered, pulled on a pair of jeans to protect against mosquitos, shimmied into a cute gauzy top to match the evening's gentle breeze, and joined her hosts at the dude ranch café. She gawked at the colors and textures of the beauty around her. It was so different from what she enjoyed about the city. In the city, she counted on colorful strangers on the bus ride to and from work, outrageously expensive and creative fashions boldly displayed in freshly washed storefronts on plastic mannequins, discordant music flowing from apartment windows, the smells of pastries wafting from the bakeries, fresh brewed coffee, and brilliant cut flowers on street corners. Here, green grasses framed the ruggedly beautiful Badlands with their subtle, yet striking, layers of colors and alternating plateaued, spired, and domed hills standing against the dramatic sky, blazing in the rich color of the setting sun. She smiled as the sounds of laughter and chatter swelled over the chirps of crickets and cattle calling in the distance.

In the dining room, Angela sat at the only empty seat she could find. The table of ten included two couples from southern California on their first ranch experience and their first trip to South Dakota.

The woman to Angela's left was quiet but seemed to silently calculate every move in the room, every cedar joint on the walls, and every opportunity to be displeased with her stay. To break the silence, and cut through the woman's mind chatter, Angela held out a hand. She had a knack for making conversation, and was curious about what was going on in this tablemate's head. "Hi, I'm Angela. How are you liking your stay so far?"

Sliding her hand into Angela's and letting it rest there while Angela pumped both hands up and down, the woman leaned in and whispered, "I'm Isabel. Do you know where I could get a stiff martini and a dreamy pool boy? Dudley, my husband, loves this nature stuff, but I miss the spa."

Angela did her best the rest of the evening to soothe Isabel's disgruntled pores. She found the secret stash of hard liquor that the dude ranch wasn't licensed to sell and made Isabel a martini, or three. By the end of the night, Angela, Bella, and Isabel were swapping stories like besties.

"Well, I know I have a baby who needs me to feed her. I'm going up to the house. Isabel, can we walk you to your cabin?" Bella felt the telltale tightness of her full breasts and knew if she didn't feed Annie soon, she would be drenched in breastmilk.

Isabel reached out her hands for her two new friends to pull her up from the chair. "You ladies have been so sweet to me. Please don't let Dudley know about those last few martinis. He prefers that I stop at one. And Bella, I really do admire what you're doing here, and your food is fabulous. I just don't prefer living so close to the dirt."

"Thank you, Isabel. I never thought I would love it here either, but it would take a lot for me to leave now. You let us know if you need anything before you leave tomorrow." The trio arrived at Isabel's cabin. As they opened the door to let Isabel in, Dudley's loud snoring greeted them.

"Are you going to be okay? Do you need our help?" Angela, the nurse, was always on duty.

"I've got this, honey. Thanks again for the evening. You both made it bearable." Isabel reached for the wall to steady herself as she stumbled over the threshold.

"Well, good night then," Bella and Angela whispered in unison then locked arms and raced for the house, stifling giggles as they moved.

"So grateful that we don't need alcohol to drown our misery. Don't get me wrong, I enjoy a nice glass of wine, but how does one allow themselves to get so miserable?" Angela pulled Bella in closer and put her arm around her shoulder. "I, for one, am so happy to be here with you, in this beautiful place, with your beautiful family."

"Honey, I know. I have missed you so and we are so glad you could come see us again."

"Well, as Annie's godmother I couldn't possibly miss out on her christening. And you picked the perfect weekend to schedule it, with the Buffalo Ridge celebration. Who knows, maybe I'll meet the cowboy of my dreams."

"From your lips to God's ears." Bella blew a kiss to the sky.

3

———

"Good morning, Miss Bella."

"Good morning, ma'am."

"Morning," a kind-faced older gentleman joined in the chorus of greetings while others nodded as Bella, Annie, and Angela passed the table of local farmers and ranchers gathered for morning coffee and gossip session.

"Good morning, gentlemen. It's great to see you all looking so fine. You must be celebrating that early morning rain we got today. I'd like you to meet my friend Angela. You might have met her before, at our wedding."

Meade, the apparent spokesperson of the group, stood and reached his enormous hand out to Angela. "On behalf of the coffee club, welcome to Buffalo Ridge. My apologies if we met before, but at eighty-two, my memory isn't quite what it used to be."

Angela returned the handshake eagerly. With a flirty smile, her bright blue eyes melded with Meade's and each of his comrades around the table. "Gentlemen, it's my pleasure to meet you, even if it is my second time. You see, I, too, suffer from memory loss. That wedding, well, it was some party."

Collectively the group chuckled and responded, "Yes, indeed it was."

"Are you staying out here in our country for a bit?"

"I'll be here two weeks this time. Each time I come, I find it harder and harder to go back to the rat race in Manhattan. You folks always make me feel at home, especially the Davies family. They are super sweet, and their door is always open."

"And you can't beat Yvette's world-class lasagna. I hope she gave you some of that. I always look forward to it when she brings it to the church socials." Orlie appeared to be the oldest of the coffee club. His still-bright blue eyes, framed by laugh lines, glistened under a sweat-stained ball cap.

"I have begged her for that recipe, but she just won't write it down for me. 'Dump and pour whatever you have that goes with ground beef and noodles,' she says." Angela shrugged her shoulders and held her hand out for the fellas to give her a clue.

"That's exactly what she told the wife when she asked," Orlie giggled.

Angela turned to follow Bella to their table, paused, and turned back to smile at the locals. This kind of small-town intimacy was unheard of in the big city. She had a half-dozen friends in the apartment building and, of course, Joel the loving doorman. There was the occasional date or wedding. She didn't fraternize much with her work family, save for one dear co-worker with whom she had worked for a long time. With most co-workers, work was all they seemed to talk about, and that was not her idea of fun.

Angela slid into the tufted black leather booth across from Bella. "Let me hold that sleeping beauty, will ya? I want to breathe in her peacefulness and watch her purse those little lips. Don't you ever wonder what she's dreaming about?"

Bella passed the sleeping bundle of joy across the table to the open arms of her godmother. "I've spent so many hours watching her. I delight in every smile, wince, and thoughtful look. I'm happy to let you gaze. It might soften you to the idea of having your own."

"Do we have to have that talk again? I love children. You know I do, but I was not well-prepared to learn the art of parenting. My house was chaos growing up, and I am scared to death of creating the same for my own child, because that's all I know."

"Oh, honey. One thing I know for sure at this point in my parenting adventure is that we don't have to repeat the mistakes of our parents. We can read about parenting, listen to real parents on podcasts, surround ourselves with people whose parenting relationships we admire, and most importantly, make a commitment to parent from the heart. I know you could do it and love it."

"Well, I know I could take this sweet little bundle home and love her 'til the cows come home. Isn't that what you say around here?" Angela stroked Annie's smooth chubby cheek and gently snugged the receiving blanket around her to keep away the cool air of the overhead fan. "Now, can we talk about the agenda? I'm sure there's bunches of stuff to do. Where do we go and how can I help?"

"You're right. There's a lot of stuff going on this weekend. On Sunday, Yvette will have a big meal with friends and neighbors after church. There's really nothing for us to do for that. We tried not to book the dude ranch too full once we got the date from Pastor Trevor, but we still have a few cabins rented. I've cooked some things ahead..."

"You broke your cardinal rule of serving frozen food? I can't believe..."

"Hey, no judgment! One thing pregnancy and parenting teaches you is flexibility. It's all good food and I tested the recipes after freezing and reheating them to make sure they met my standards. They're good and I need the time for other priorities. This year I will participate in the town celebration activities. I really look forward to it, and so does Marco."

"What are some of the activities he can do?"

"Steve's been working with him on the … hiya Brenda, how you doin'?" A fifty-something woman with a cook's cap raced by and patted Bella's arm with a greeting. "That's Brenda, she makes the doughnuts fresh here every morning. A great gal with a wild story, best left for evening chatter." Bella reached out to pat Annie. "Now where was I?"

"Steve worked with Marco on what?" Angela kept her gaze on Annie, hoping she would open her eyes and look into hers.

"Mutton bustin'."

"What is that, anyway?"

"Well, the kids try to ride a sheep for eight seconds. It's kinda like kindergarten bull riding, I guess. This will be the last year Marco can ride…he's getting too big. He barely made it this year, but thanks to his Italian genes he's pretty light yet."

"I'm sorry Bella, but that just sounds like animal cruelty… making those little lambs carry those kids on their backs."

"I hear ya. Not only that, but we paid $20 so Marco can participate. The thing is, it's part of the way of life here and a way to introduce the younger kids to rodeo."

"Now, don't get me start…"

Bella nodded her head in agreement and held her hand up to stop Angela's protest. "Rodeo is a big deal around here. I know it's easy to judge it as being cruel to animals and dangerous for people, but again, it's a way of life here and not to have it would be like tearing the Statue of Liberty down or closing Ellis Island to visitors. It would just change everything about the culture and community."

"Well, if you say so. I still get squirmy about all of it, but of course, I will go watch the little man."

"He would be shattered if you didn't. You probably also want to see him fighting through the straw pile trying to find quarters."

"That sounds like quite a mess."

"It is, and the kids love it."

"Can they find enough quarters to do anything with?"

"Now, that's a great question. Can't do much with a quarter, so we match whatever he gets so he can buy candy or something at the rodeo in the evening."

"Wait, so now there's riding lambs, digging in straw and a rodeo?"

"Oh, Ang…there's so much more." Bella paused to wave at yet another friend, who marched to where they were sitting.

"Well, you have that baby out in these crowds?!" she scolded.

"Hello Martha. Yes, I sure do, and look how peacefully she's sleeping."

"Well now, just let me see that princess's face." Martha reached past Angela to spread the blanket open and see the baby. "Oh, my, she is the most beautiful thing, just like a porcelain doll my momma used to have in the attic."

Bella nearly spit her water across the table. "Oh, how sweet," she mumbled, barely audible. "Martha, you may remember my friend…"

"That's right, well, if it isn't Angela. I remember you. We don't get a lot of peaches and cream complexion with red hair around here. Our redheads are more ruddy. I just remember you standing up there with Bella when she got married and thought, now ain't she just like one of momma's dolls. Like that one in the box that never got touched."

"It's a pleasure to see you again, Martha. Did you get a good look at the baby?"

"Sure did. Now, you cover her back up and let her sleep. It's gonna get wild 'round here soon and she should be rested…" Martha turned to Bella, put her hand on her hip and declared, "or at home away from the crowds."

"I'll take that under advisement, Martha. But surely, we will see you in church on Sunday, right? That's Annie's big christening day."

"Wouldn't miss it for the world. You know that."

"Well great! If we don't see you before then, have a great celebration weekend."

"Surely will do that, I will. Surely will. Now you gals take care of that little one and her big brother. What a sweet boy he is." Martha scratched her greying pin curls with calloused fingers and looked over her shoulder. "I gotta find Earl and get us back home. Boys will be needing their lunch in the fields soon. Bye girls."

Martha raced away as quickly as she rushed in, hell-bent on getting the boys fed.

4

"How did you ladies do in town?" Steve stood beside the pickup and patted his jeans, causing clouds of dust to fly into the air.

"Lots of love in the community for your little princess here." Angela unbuckled baby Annie from the car seat and gently held her. "We tried to have a visit, but person after person stopped by to love on her."

"You can't beat small towns for caring about their families, that's for sure. It can get a bit challenging to find your own space amongst all those who want to support you, but I wouldn't have it any other way." Steve reached into the pickup and pulled out a pair of leather work gloves. "Bella, I need to fix some fence over there south of Shorty's. I'll be back in a couple hours. The bunkhouses are all turned over and ready for guests. We'll be full again tonight and there's only one special request for dinner. Seems we have a guest celebrating his 50th birthday, and his wife said he loves chocolate."

"Perfect. I've got a new chocolate raspberry marquise recipe I want to experiment with. Is Marco going with you?"

"He sure is. I sent him in to put boots on. Snakes are out."

On cue, Marco raced down the steps to the pickup, but

made a sharp turn to give Angela a hug. "Did I tell you yet how happy I am to see you?"

Angela looked down into his big dark eyes. "You can just keep telling me, handsome. I'm so happy to be here with you. You're going to go help your dad now, right? Later, will you tell me all about the rodeo and the sheep riding?"

"You mean mutton busting? Of course. We can talk later, Auntie." Marco turned to Steve, "Come on Dad. Let's get this work done so we can get back here."

"You heard the man," chuckled Steve. "We're going to work now. I'll see you three later. Mom can't wait to catch up with you, Angela. She's so excited you're here."

"I'll find her and pour us a cup. Yvette always has some great stories to share."

DUST SPUN UPWARD to meet the gauzy clouds passing through the brilliant sky as the pickup faded from view on the country road.

"I'm going to feed and change the baby. You're free to do what you wa…Ange? Are you okay?" Bella moved closer and put a hand on Angela's shoulder.

"Oh, never mind me. I'm such a softy, you know. It's just seeing you so happy and Marco doing so well. I think about how much you would have missed if you didn't take that brave journey out west." Angela turned to Bella and leaned in, touching her head gently against Bella's. "These are tears of joy. Really, they are. You couldn't have had this if you stayed in the city."

"Oh, hun. I do love it here so, and Steve is such a wonderful partner. I just know you will have a happily ever after, too, someday."

The two walked out of the summer heat. "Sorry the house is a mess. I'm still adjusting to having a little one."

"Bella, your house is perfect. I honestly don't see how you do everything, including work, with a new baby. Wouldn't you just love a little time off?"

"That's the thing that really works here. There's family close enough to help out, and they all know how much it means to me to cook and serve our guests. It's like I'm bringing them pleasure in ways they don't expect out here on the prairie. There's something about it for me. It's like I get as much as I give and it revives me. Besides, Yvette is so great at pitching in, whether it's holding the baby while I work or helping in the kitchen."

"Speaking of Yvette, I'll freshen up a bit and join her. I think I saw her car at the café."

"Hey, before you go, we never did finish talking about the agenda for this weekend. Tomorrow is the kids' mutton busting at eight in the morning." She giggled at the mocked horror on Angela's face. "I know, I know, that's early. The parade is at eleven on Main St., kids' games, food trucks, and ice cream social right after, the rodeo in the early evening, and then the beer tent and dance downtown. We will go to the nine o'clock service on Sunday morning for Annie's baptism, and then there will be a family dinner at Yvette's."

"Oh wow! Busy times! Are Steve's siblings all going to make it? Would be fun to see them again."

"Stella can't make it, but Jesse, Kerry, Chance, and Pauline will be there. I don't know who else Yvette may have invited." Bella settled into the rocker with baby Annie ready for nursing. "There is something magical about this time I get with Annie, where she is totally dependent on me, yet it feels nothing like a burden. It's an irreplaceable exchange of energy we have, where she gives me as much as I give her."

Angela kicked pebbles off the flagstones as she walked down the gentle slope from the house to the dude ranch, waving to the staff in the greenhouse as she passed by. Further down the path she passed the stable, where an unfamiliar hired hand was cleaning and putting away the tack after a morning trail ride.

"Hey there, I'm Angela, a friend of…"

The handsome young man tipped his hat, pulled off his leather glove and held his hand out to Angela. "Bella and Steve's. I'm pleased to meet you ma'am. There's been a lot of excitement about your visit here. Marco has been talking non-stop about his Auntie Angie."

"That's sweet. And you are…"

"My apologies, ma'am. I'm Clint. I'm working this summer before I head back to college. I help with the trail rides, and some other things that need to be done on the ranch."

"Clint, it's my pleasure to meet you. I'm sure we'll be seeing one another again. Maybe I can even join one of your trail rides."

"Sure, you can. Any time you want to. Would be nice to have you along."

Yvette was setting the tables for dinner when Angela entered the dude ranch café. She stopped to offer a warm welcoming hug. "There you are, you beautiful girl! I've been beside myself with excitement to see you. Come in, tell me all about what's going on in that big city life of yours."

Angela knew that if she started talking about her life, Yvette would interrupt to share news from Buffalo Ridge. She preempted Yvette, "No, you first. I know you have had lots of visitors and have been working hard down here at the dude ranch. You tell me. How's it going?"

Yvette easily filled the next half hour, getting Angela caught up on local gossip, the family, the dude ranch, and plans for a winter cruise with her husband, Dan. "And, we have a new pastor at the church, Trevor Phillips. Now there's a story for you. Anyway, I'm sure you'll meet him this weekend. Nice young man."

"That sounds intriguing. We'll have to find some more time to chat. For now, what can I do to help out around here?"

5

———

"Hang on, Marco, don't let him throw you off! That's right, hang on…" Angela's cheers were interrupted by the loud sound of a buzzer followed by the roar of the crowd and booming voice of an excited announcer.

"There you have it folks! Marco Davies, the last rider for the event, has made it to the eight-second buzzer, and what a beautiful ride it was. Way to go Marco! Your daddy Steve, once a mutton bustin' champion himself, is gonna help you back out of the arena. Folks, we have a score of 89 for young Mister Davies, making him the top rider today. There he is, pulling his helmet off and showing you that handsome grin. Give the boy a round of applause. He's a future rodeo cowboy, right there."

Marco held his helmet under his arm as he waved to the crowd; his grin widened when he spotted Angela and the rest of his family.

"That was a good ride, right?" Angela didn't want to feel invested in this sport that disadvantaged an animal, but she would always be a supporter of Marco. She knew the turmoil he was born into, with a hard-working mom overcoming childhood poverty and family loss, and a philandering dad who did not marry Bella or provide financial support, despite his undeniable means.

"That was the best, and a fantastic way to end his mutton busting career. Next year he will move into some other events that require more technical skills, like roping." Bella knew that Marco would be involved in goat tying, but didn't want to alarm Angela.

A man, passing behind them in the bleachers, paused and rested his broad hand on Bella's shoulder. He was an aging man, with a sun-etched face featuring striking high cheekbones and dark eyes, suggesting he was likely a member of one of the state's Native American tribes. His kind eyes twinkled. "Well, now, Bella, that boy is representing the Davies family well. I bet you're a proud momma this morning."

"Hey thank you, Walt. I sure am proud. Good to see you. I saw McKayla out there giving it her best. She's one tough little girl, that one."

"Oh yes," Walt chuckled softly. "Of all my grandkids, and I have twelve of them, she's the most defiant, and if she decides to be a rodeo princess, it'll serve her well. If it doesn't, I guess her mom and dad are going to have to put one of those GPS devices on her to keep track of her."

He nodded to the rest of the Davies family, now gathered together in the bleachers awaiting the arrival of the star of the show. "And there he is. Hey son, you're looking a lot like your uncle Chance out there. Give me a high-five for that great performance you put on."

Marco met Walt's hand with a sharp high-five strike. "Thank you, Mr. Walt. Dad did most of my training with me, but Uncle Chance gave me some pointers, and I think they helped."

"Well, it looked like it all came together for you out there." Walt turned to his wife, Trudy, and took her hand in his. "We're going to head on downtown for the parade and other fun things. Got all the grandkids up off the ranches today.

We'll see how they get along. You all have a fun time at the celebration."

"I'll give you a call, Yvette," Trudy said while passing, "to talk about the kids clothing drive."

"Sounds perfect, Trude. I've got some ideas for new donors, so I'm excited to get started." Yvette raised her free hand and wiggled the fingers in a gentle wave. "I'm sure we'll see you again downtown."

As Yvette would later explain, Walt was a kind and encouraging soul. He and Trudy were known around the area as foster parents to kids on the reservations who needed care. Walt was especially skilled at turning troubled teens around, while Trudy, a nurse, could handle the babies who needed special care. Trudy and Yvette had worked on many projects throughout the county over the years. Neither of them did it for the glory, but for the good they knew they were doing for others.

ANGELA JOINED the Davies family for the parade, the kids' games, lunch and the ice cream social. They treated her like one of the family. As someone whose own family was dysfunctional and distant, this was a gift of immeasurable value. With her striking beauty and always fashionable style, Angela stood out in the crowd and attracted attention. The Davies family shielded her from those who were just curious, but graciously introduced her to their friends. With each visit to Buffalo Ridge, Angela felt more welcomed into the fold of the small town.

"Marco, what did you think about the marching band in the parade?" Angela could see that Marco was gulping down lunch as fast as he could in order to join friends back at the bouncy house. She wanted him to pause a moment and cool off under the misting tent.

"You're funny, Auntie. They weren't marching. They were sitting on haybales on a flatbed trailer."

"You're right. Did you like the music?"

"Sure, I guess. I mostly just like the parade for the candy and the firetrucks."

"Is that right? Well, I bet one day you'll be in that parade and then maybe you will see it differently."

Marco shrugged and asked to be excused to throw away the lunch trash and join his friends.

"See you, Auntie. I'm just going over there with Cole and Cash." Marco pointed to the end of the block where the inflatable games stood.

Angela smiled. "See you later, Marco."

<hr>

BY MID-AFTERNOON the group had visited with half the town, participated in all the activities, and felt exhausted; but there were still chores to do.

"Well, my friends, Dan and I are going to swing by the café and see that the girls are set for dinner tonight." Yvette was the veritable traffic cop, keeping the whole family's cogs in motion. "Bella and Angela, are you going to take the kids home and regroup? And Angela, you and I can hang out later with the princess while the rest go to the rodeo. Dan is going to check on the cows while I make a salad for tomorrow and make sure I've got enough clean di…"

"You know Mom, we can have everyone come to the café for lunch tomorrow if you want."

"Thanks, Steve, but I really want this to be at the house tomorrow. No offense, but it just seems a little more personal that way."

"We understand. Just let us know what we can do."

"I'll tell you what you can do. You can have a good time

tonight, show up for church on time tomorrow, and eat well, because I have enough food for an army."

The group went their own direction, with a promise to meet up after the rodeo before the dance. Only Dan and Yvette, with baby Annie, would not attend the dance. Still obviously in love after nearly four decades of marriage, Dan draped his arm around Yvette. "We've done our late-night dancing. Now it's you all's turn to kick up the dust. And kids, make sure our Angela has a great time, too, will ya?"

In unison, the Davies kids and their spouses affirmed their intent to do just that.

"That depends. Can you two-step?" Chance nudged Angela with an elbow.

"As a matter of fact smarty-pants, I had a co-worker show me how in the parking garage of the hospital. I think I can do it, at least a little." Angela loved dancing and studied it some in college, so she was confident in her ability to catch on quickly, even if she didn't have all the moves down right away.

6

"What did you think of our little town's celebration?" Yvette and Angela sat on the deck of the older Davies' home looking out over the rim of the Badlands.

"So far it's been a lot of fun. It seems like the locals really get into the celebration and use it as a time to meet up with friends they may not see often. And those class reunions. Wow, they go back to the beginning of time! There were two people in the parade that graduated seventy years ago!"

Angela had not been to a high school class reunion, including the ten-year reunion. Her graduating class was larger than the entire population of Buffalo Ridge. Even so, while in school she didn't really have any close friends. Her home life was unstable and embarrassing. Her commitment to do well in school, in order to earn a college scholarship, consumed her, as did the part-time job stocking shelves at the neighborhood grocer. She avoided being at home, where she was alone for long periods of time while her parents pursued their careers and avoided one another. Nor did she want to be around to witness their loveless marriage, arguments, brooding and loneliness. Her siblings were older and out of the house by the time Angela entered high school, leaving her to fend for herself.

Yvette rocked Annie as she talked. "Funny thing is, those two fellas who graduated seventy years ago are cousins. Both are bachelors who live on farms that are side by side. Hardly a reunion at all for them. They probably see each other at the mailbox every day."

The two women chuckled at the apparent absurdity of the reunion, then fell into silence, each contemplating their own past and potential reunions. Annie woke with a tiny cry, propelling Angela into action, warming a bottle, while Yvette soothed the baby with a snuggle and song.

"You know, Angela, it's eight-thirty already. Please go! I'm good here with Annie. Take my car into town. Park over by the bank and then just walk across the street to the tent. That's where the dance is. Just bring my car back tomorrow, that's fine. We've got pickups we can use for church." Having been changed and fed, the baby was once again asleep in grandma's arms.

"Is there anything else you want me to do to prepare for tomorrow? I hate that you are doing all the work. I'm not a wizard in the kitchen like Bella is, but I follow directions well."

A helper at heart, Angela had passion, and her soul was fed by making life easier or enhanced for others. She once was in therapy after a breakup; a man, who she believed she was deeply in love with, left suddenly for another woman. She learned in that process that she was a people-pleaser, found joy in serving others, but often at her own expense. While she was aware of this tendency, she didn't really know how to be anything else and had not trained herself to be anything but a helper. As a result, she was scared to plunge deeply into romantic relationships, for fear she was doing it wrong.

"No, we are in great shape for tomorrow. You go on out and have yourself a great time. I would say 'let your hair down' but your hair is perfect, and you look so cute with your boots and skirt. I would bet that your feet will be screaming at you tomorrow."

"I'll keep you posted on that," Angela said as she tapped her shiny new boots together. "You have my number. Call if you need anything, and I mean it."

"You're so sweet. Dan will be home soon. Annie and I will just enjoy the sunset and then the stars. You have a beautiful night to go out and play. Now, go kick up your heels and report back tomorrow."

<hr>

ANGELA FELT her hand being tugged as a handsome cowboy about her age pulled her out onto the dance floor. She quickly tucked the car keys into a shirt pocket and let the man lead her around the dance floor, two-stepping faster than she thought possible.

"Wow, that was quite a workout." Angela caught her breath while the new friend introduced himself.

"I've done faster, but yeah, that was a good clip. This is a great band for dancing country. I'm Justen. You're Bella's friend. Angel, is it?"

"Angela. Nice to meet you, Justen. You're really good at this."

"Aw, thanks. I've been country dancing since I was as little as that one over there." Justen pointed to a small boy, maybe five or six years old.

"This is my first dance doing the two-step." Angela didn't feel the need to go into the parking lot rehearsals at the hospital before coming out west.

"You did great! My gal's a barrel racer. She's on her way over here, so I had better be on the look-out for her. We'll check on you later. You're probably waiting for the Davies clan. I see Jesse and Kerry coming in now. I'm sure the rest will follow soon if they aren't already here." Justen shook Angela's hand, thanked her for the dance and headed toward the entrance to await his girlfriend.

Angela waved to Jesse and Kerry and spotted Bella in line.

"Hey guys, good to see you. I've been warming up the dance floor for ya. Me and Justen, over there." Angela ran her hand through her hair, trying to smooth the wisps that strayed while she was on the dance floor.

"Yeah, we caught the tail end of that. I had no idea you could move like that. I thought you would prefer disco-style dancing." Jesse smiled the charming Davies smile, and motioned for Angela to follow he and Kerry to the concessions. "Can I buy you a drink?"

"Sure, I'll have a bottle of water. Seems I'm going to need to stay hydrated to get through this night."

"Why don't you grab that empty table over there and I'll bring it over. Looks like it's about big enough for our crew." Jesse pointed across the room and motioned for Kerry to go with Angela. The rest of the Davies family soon followed.

———

"KERRY, how are you? We haven't had any time to catch up. How's the practice?" Kerry was just getting a veterinary practice established when Angela first met her. At that time, she was taking every call and had no backup.

"It's great, and now I have a new grad who has come on board to help me. We are expanding our building, so we have more boarding options." Kerry's dream of having her own practice had come true, with tremendous support from Jesse. A true Davies through and through, he was steadfast and faithful. "I couldn't ask for anything more."

"Here we are, a round of waters. Big drinkers, aren't we?" Jesse placed an armload of plastic water bottles on the picnic table. He turned his attention to Marco, dressed in black from his boots to his hat. "So buddy, what did you like best at the big rodeo?"

Marco answered without taking his eyes off the band and the dance floor. "That's easy. Bull riding, of course." He threw a look over his shoulder to Chance as he answered the question. "You should know that. I'm a Davies."

The group laughed and nodded.

"That's right, boy, and don't you forget it. You're a Davies and you're gonna be a rodeo star," Chance retorted. "Now get your skinny little self out there and show those kids how to dance."

Angela accepted dance invitations from each of the Davies men as the evening progressed. Not typically one for too much male attention, Angela focused on the challenge of the dance and keeping up with her partners.

She found that Chance, despite the many mended bones in his bull rider's body, was the most athletic on the dance floor and the most fun. As they exited the dance floor, a tall, dark man with a beaming smile, kind eyes and chiseled body reached out for Chance's hand and shook it heartily. "You two looked like you had years of practice. Chance, nice to see you."

He turned to Angela. "I think you must be Angela. Hi, I'm Trevor." He held his hand out to her. "It's nice to meet you at last. I've heard so much about you."

Looking at the handsome stranger in front of her, Angela's breath caught in her throat and her mouth went dry as she became lost in this experience of city slicker meeting sophisticated and ruggedly gorgeous cowboy. She wiped her hand on her skirt to dissipate the dance sweat that lingered there and placed it in Trevor's.

"I am she…uh…Angela." Captivated by his eyes and smile, Angela, uncharacteristically, was at a loss for words. She absorbed the warmth and strength of his hand, without trying to impress this new acquaintance with the firm grip of the fiercely independent and strong woman she thought she was.

"It's great to finally meet you. Marco has been telling me all about your visit to see the baby." Trevor paused a moment before releasing Angela's hand and excused himself. "I'm sorry to meet and run, but my curfew has arrived and it's time for me to head home. I'll see you folks again real soon." He backed away, with his eyes fixed on Angela's, until he collided with a two-stepper, then raised his hand in farewell, turned and disappeared into the crowd.

Angela spun around to find Chance back out on the dance floor with Pauline, twirling her like a pro. Pauline had all the moves and looked completely carefree with dark hair flying behind her. Angela returned to the Davies table to find that Jesse and Kerry had already left, and Bella, clutching her milk-bound breasts, was preparing to leave with Steve. Aware of tomorrow's early morning plans, and feeling like she may never be able to peel her sweaty feet from those fancy cowgirl boots if she kept dancing, Angela decided it was time to leave as well.

"Guys, I'm ready to cash it in. I'm going to leave right now so I can call dibs on the shower. I know you have to stop and pick up Annie." Angie looked at her watch. It was ten fifteen. "Hey Marco, it's waaaay past your bedtime. Do you want to ride home with me? We have an early morning tomorrow."

Marco didn't want to leave, but knew he had to, and riding home with Angie made it a bit easier. He wanted to talk to her about the rodeo and the dance. "Can I, Mom?"

"Of course, you can. Why don't you take a quick shower and rinse off the rodeo arena dust? We won't really have time to do that in the morning. Your clothes are all laid out for church." Bella kissed her son's sweaty head. "Sleep well, my love."

7

*A*ngela felt the sunlight creeping in around the window shades before she saw it. She was parched and still tired after a restless night. After tossing and turning into the wee hours of the morning, she had finally fallen into a deep sleep and probably had dreamt but didn't recall. Her phone face showed 7:13, more than an hour after she planned to be up to help the family get ready for the early church service. She bounded out of bed, threw on her church dress and raced to the bathroom, where she found Marco brushing his teeth.

"Good morning sleepyhead." Marco's broad smile was punctuated by toothpaste remnants.

"Why didn't you get me up? I wanted to make you breakfast." Angela leaned against the doorframe, waiting for Marco to finish.

"Mom said to let you sleep. Besides, grandma made breakfast. Mom just had to warm it up this morning."

"Your grandma is something else, I tell ya. Are you done in there so I can beautify this morning?"

"You're already beautiful, Auntie. You don't need that make-up stuff to be beautiful." Marco wiped his mouth and approached the doorway.

Angela shared a warm hug with him. "You are my very special little man, Marco. You really know how to make a girl feel special. Now, off with you so I can get ready."

———

WHEN ANGELA EMERGED from the bathroom a short time later, her hair was perfect, each eyelash was coated in mascara and lipstick flawlessly accented her perfect mouth.

"Well, aren't you the picture of perfection." Bella stood in her robe, having just fed the baby. "Would you please take her while I get ready? Her christening gown is there on the rocker. Do you think you could put it on her?"

"Of course. Good morning baby girl. Let's get you ready, shall we?" Angela took the sleeping beauty into her arms. "Hey Bella, do you know a guy, a tall dark and handsome guy, named Trevor?"

"Yeah, I sure do. Nice guy." Bella moved toward the bedroom to get ready. They needed to be out the door in twenty minutes. She turned to Steve, who was shining up the boots he reserved for special occasions. "I don't know why we agreed to the early service, hun."

Steve turned to Bella. "You are so beautiful, babe, and the most wonderful wife and mother. Just stand there a minute in the sunlight while I take you in." He stood and moved toward Bella, wrapping his arms around her, and kissed the top of her head. "Early service because there's wheat to harvest and hay to mow, I think is what we said. It'll be fine. You could show up in your robe and still be the most beautiful woman in the world."

Bella rested her head on Steve's chest for a moment. "You are my Mr. Wonderful, in every sense."

Pausing a moment, Bella looked up as Steve bent and met her lips with his. "I'm the luckiest man alive."

As this beautiful, loving scene unfolded before her, Angela

felt a tug at her heart and tears threatening to ruin the fresh morning make-up. Marco, on the other hand, was not so impressed. "Okay! Okay! Enough with the kisses!" And then, deepening his little voice in an attempt to imitate the rodeo announcer, he announced, "Let's get this show rolling…or jumping…or whatever."

Laughter filled the room. Now warm and calm, Bella headed off to get dressed. Steve announced that he and Marco would take Yvette's car, and Bella would drive Angela and Annie to the church.

"That's a great plan. Cover for me if I'm running a little late, will ya?" Bella called out.

"Good morning. Welcome. Oh, is this the precious child of Christ being baptized this morning?"

Without further ado, the greeter ushered the family to the front pew. The other Davies families were already in their places in the pew behind them.

"Phew. It's 8:57 and we're seated." Bella looked at Angela seated next to her. "Oh Ange, dear me! She spit up a little bit on your beautiful dress."

Angela looked down to see a small spot of curdled breastmilk on her royal blue dress. "Oh, let me just run to the restroom real quick." Angela handed Annie to Bella and shuffled down the outside row and toward the narthex.

The Pastor entered the sanctuary and looked out upon the crowd gathered for the early morning service. "Good morning! It's great to see everyone gathered here this morning for this very special service."

Trevor paused to scan the front pews carefully. "It's not

often we have a full house at the early service this time of year, with all the demands of your farms and ranches, but as we welcome a new child of God…" Trevor paused again - his eyes locked on Angela, as she carefully and quietly made her way across the nave to the front pew. She looked up and froze when her eyes met his.

The tall, dark, handsome man from the night before was leading the service? *Maybe he is filling in as the pastor*, she thought. Suddenly conscious of the wet spot just created on her dress, she put her hand above her breast to cover it. Realizing she had interrupted the service, Angela smiled at the congregation before continuing to the front pew. *Oh, why did they have to be in the front?*

"Yes, we welcome a new child of God…and her special friends…" Trevor paused and nodded slightly, again holding Angela's eyes with his, "…and family to this special service." Holding up the service bulletin, Trevor spoke to the congregation. "You can refer to the bulletin for upcoming events and later, Lilian will give us a report on the ice cream social. I do know it was a big hit as many people sought me out to share about the good time they had, so thank you to Phoebe's group for once again hosting this successful event. Now, I invite you to please greet one another and then Rhonda will lead us in our first hymn, 'There is a Fountain Filled with Blood', which will be displayed overhead so you can join in."

Angela moved slowly as she greeted Marco, Yvette, and Dan, with a head awhirl with questions. Her stomach churned with energy that could find no home, as she tried to reconcile the tall, dark, and handsome Trevor, whose presence stunned her the night before, and the man standing at the altar. Lost in thought, Angela preoccupied herself with the baby, occasionally singing a line or joining in on the responsive prayers, until she felt an elbow in her ribs.

"Angela, come on. It's time for the baptism." Bella urged

Angela to rise and follow her to the front of the congregation, where Trevor was waiting to perform the baptism ceremony.

In a fog of scattered thought, Angela heard herself say "I will" when prompted, and recite the words printed in the bulletin for her. The weight of the words did not hit her until the moment when she affirmed, in front of the congregation and Trevor, that she would see that Annie was raised with religious training and knowledge of the triune God if her parents were unable to. The gravity of that promise hit her in the gut. She made a mental note to learn more about how she could fulfill those duties if, God forbid, she ever had to. Until that moment, Angela relied on childhood memories of baptism associated with finery and joy. The parents and godparents wore their finest clothes, the baby wore a delicate, custom hand-stitched gown, and there was talk of champagne celebrations and finger food afterwards.

In adult life, Angela dabbled in church but never committed to a church home, always making herself available to work on Sundays to allow other nurses with families the opportunity to go to church. The veil of childlike thinking was lifted, and she was suddenly awake to the opportunity and obligations of being an adult in worship.

As anticipated, the greetings in the narthex after the service were joyous and celebratory. Friends and strangers alike gushed over the baby, and excitedly invited Angela to morning coffee, evening bar-b-ques and the weekly women's softball game. Through it all, Angela kept an eye on Trevor, and when he approached the baptism receiving line, she ducked out.

"Annie needs a diaper. I'm just going to change her real quick before we go. I'll meet you at the car," Angela whispered to Bella, who nodded, unaware of Angela's angst.

8

---

ngela was initially quiet on the ride to Yvette and Dan's, preoccupied with a cascade of thoughts, starting with Trevor and ending with questions about her role in religion and feelings about spirituality. She felt an existential crisis coming on, but wanted to be fully present with Bella, Annie and the rest of the family.

"So, Bella, remember I asked you about Trevor earlier this morning?"

"Yeah, so what do you think? Nice guy, huh?"

"Well, I thought so last night, but why didn't you tell me he was your preacher?!"

"Last night? What do you mean?"

"Well, I was dancing with Chance, who is a fantastic two-stepper by the way, and along came this gorgeous man with a smile that melted my heart. We talked only briefly, but I was just star-struck and felt, deep in my soul, that this is someone I really wanted to get to know better."

"I think that's great Ange, but you don't seem as excited about it now. You actually look a little tortured." Bella took one hand off the steering wheel and rested it on Angela's for a moment.

"I am more than a little tortured. I mean, a preacher? You know I'm not super religious. Heck, my church for years has been the ER. My favorite preachers are the hospital chaplains that deliver last rites. I mean, what do I know about church and religion, except what I experienced as a child? Besides, preachers don't date…do they?"

"Woah, girl! Slow your roll a bit here. Trevor is a man. A very nice man with an interesting past. His job is that of a preacher, it is not all of who he is. I actually think, whether there's a romantic future or not, he is someone you would like to get to know. Just think of it as meeting a new friend."

"Well, I don't know. We'll see. I may never see him again, especially if I skip church next Sunday."

"First, it's a small town, so you are likely to see him again. Second, nobody will force you to go to church. And third, I know you'll see him again soon."

"You do, huh? How so?"

"He's coming to the baptismal celebration lunch at Yvette's."

"Oh, my God, Bella! What are you doing to me? I suddenly feel sick. Can you just take me home?"

"Well, I didn't do anything to you. I didn't even invite him. That was all Yvette's doing, and I'm sure it was not to set you up, but to show appreciation for his service today. Besides, he's a friend of the family. He and Chance were in school together in Buffalo Ridge for a couple of years."

"No kidding. I didn't know he was from here."

"Well, you've got a lot to learn. Make friends, Angela. I promise you it will be worth it. He is so interesting, and you don't have to feel pressure for it to be anything else."

"Jesse and Kerry, why don't you sit here." Yvette was in her element as she organized the table. "Angela, Trevor, and Steve,

I'm going to put you on the end, opposite your father with Bella around the corner, then Marco."

Angela smiled and slowly slipped into the chair beside Kerry. She felt a gentle push helping move her chair up to the table and turned to see Trevor smiling down at her.

"May I help?"

"Uh, sure…thank you." Tucking her elbows in, Angela unfolded the napkin onto her lap and tried to make herself small, avoiding any awkward touches with tablemates.

"Yvette, you have outdone yourself!" Bella picked up the little, white, plastic baby buggy filled with candies sitting at her plate. Each guest had one.

"Oh, aren't those just fun? I know they're cheesy, but it'll give us something to talk with Annie about in years to come. I've put one in her keepsake box." Yvette sat down next to Dan. "If you can believe this, I did not make lasagna today."

The guests snickered and groaned in disappointment. Yvette was famous for her lasagna, that recipe she refused to share with even close friends and relatives.

"Instead, I have a new favorite. We have beef brisket and some homemade buns if you want to turn yours into a sandwich. There's watermelon and basil salad, pasta salad, a broccoli slaw salad and some other usual things you will recognize. We do have dessert, too, so save a little room." Yvette paused to take inventory of the food on the table and assure herself that nothing had been left in the kitchen.

"It's great to have everyone here. Well, except Stella. I know she told you, but I'll tell the table anyway, that she sends her apologies. She had hoped to come, but their hired hand got injured so she had to make the ride this week to move the cattle."

"Thanks, Mom. Bella and I do understand. She did say she hoped to see us at Christmas, if not before."

"That's right. Hopefully that beautiful baby of yours won't

be grown up by the time she gets back. She is the wild card, our Stella. Pastor… oh it seems so odd to call you that at my dining room table. You were just Trev when you ate here as a young person."

"Yvette, please call me Trev, especially here in your home. Yes, I have eaten many a wonderful meal right here. And so many late-night movies and card games when I lived in Buffalo Ridge." Trevor nodded in Chance's direction. "That fella over there saw to it that I had fun but stayed out of serious trouble. I'm forever grateful, man."

"It's mutual, Trev. It was only after you left that I really got the wild hair."

"Well, since today is Annie's special day. I wonder if you would say grace for us Trev? "

"I would be honored, Yvette." Trevor held his hands out to each of his neighbors and together the group formed a circle, with Marco holding Annie's tiny hand as she rested on Bella's lap.

"God, we thank you for this coming together of family and friends…" Trevor's smooth, confident voice lulled Angela. She followed the inflections and intonations of his voice but could not focus on the words. She flinched slightly when she felt a squeeze of her hand and then heard Trevor end the prayer.

"Amen," she uttered, uncertain of what all had been said in the prayer. She turned to Trevor and whispered, "Thank you," as the others did.

"Well now, folks, that darlin' granddaughter of ours is gonna git hungry soon, so we might as well pass around this wonderful food my beautiful bride prepared for today. If we do it quick, that baby may not wake up and realize what she is missing out on. Steve, can you help Bella fill her plate there? She's got her hands full."

Trevor approached Angela who was on the deck, enjoying a cup of coffee and the view of the prairie-framed badlands. She was admiring the rugged yet picture-perfect setting, with the greens and golds of the flat prairie set against the muted watercolor stripes of the badlands. Bella was taking care of Annie, and Yvette refused any offer to help with the clean-up. "What did you think of our little town's celebration?"

"I have to say, Trevor…uh, or is it pastor?"

"Please, call me Trevor. These people are like my family and formalities are not necessary here."

"Trevor, the celebration was a lot of fun. It's unlike anything I've ever experienced before, and of course Marco made it fun with all his activities."

"I'm glad to hear that. I agree that kids make it more fun. Since I've been back in town, in this job, it's a little different for me, but I still enjoy the opportunity to see friends, old and new alike." Trevor smiled and leaned back into his chair.

"So, you lived here before? How is it, coming back to your hometown?"

"I did live here. There was a time in my life when I lived with my grandparents. They were older and needed some help. It, uh…came at a time when my mother was super busy with her own life…uh…and we decided it would be best for me to come here and help her parents. They've both passed on now."

Trevor felt himself stumble over his story. He didn't want to disclose things to this beautiful woman that would cause her to run away before he got to know her. Chance had given him a glimpse into her life. He knew she was single and lived on the east coast. Chance described her as a workaholic with a huge heart who could be a lot of fun.

As Angela listened, a million questions popped into her head, but it was too soon to bombard this handsome man, who seemed so genuine, with questions. She could tell he was of mixed race, and assumed it was his mother who was white, coming from this part of the country. She would get more information from Steve when they were back at the dude ranch. For now, she just wanted to enjoy the day of celebration and keep it light.

"If you don't mind me asking, have you always lived on the east coast?"

"I don't mind. I'm pretty much an open book. I have a pretty boring life, actually, and yes, I was born and raised in New York state and have lived in Manhattan since I went to nursing school."

"How do you like it there?"

"It's all I ever knew, until Bella made that brave move out here and I got to come spend time with her. I realized then the gamut of lifestyles that exist from the fast-paced big city to the quiet small town."

Trevor leaned forward in his chair. "Have you found a preference yet?"

Trevor, slow your roll, he chastised himself. *Let her story unfold. Don't be in such a rush.* It had been a long time since he had allowed himself to acknowledge any feelings he had for a woman. A very long time.

Angela looked at Trevor and smiled. "I haven't ruled anything out, but there is a certain charm about small towns that can never be recreated in the city, and a level of adrenaline rush in the big city that is experienced less here on the prairie."

Playing it safe, Angela did not share how much she would like to be closer to those she considered her family of choice, Bella and Marco.

"I used to live in New York City. That's where my mom lived."

"Is that right?" Angela uncrossed her legs and stretched out sandaled feet to rest polished toes on the footstool.

"Yah. It was okay as a kid, but now that I've been away,

when I go back to New York I can get overwhelmed. Maybe it's just me getting older."

"I hear that."

Trevor looked at his cell phone and a tiny furrow etched in the otherwise smooth tawny skin between his eyes. He leaned forward in the chair with his hands on his knees and turned his head to look at Angela. "It has been great meeting you. I rarely find someone familiar with the east coast to compare notes with. I'm sorry, but I need to go visit a church member in the hospital over in Twullip. I do hope we get a chance to visit again before you leave. You have several more days here, don't you?"

"Yes, Trevor, it has been nice chatting. I will be here for ten more days and would be glad to chat more, although beyond the east coast. I would love to hear what it's been like for you to settle in here after spending a lot of time in the city."

"That sounds great."

"I'll walk you out."

Angela accompanied Trevor as he bid farewell to the family, hugging and shaking hands with each one.

Yvette held out a shopping bag bulging with containers of leftovers. "I have a care package for you."

"Thank you, Yvette. Did you, by chance, add some of that wonderful dessert in there?" He embraced her like a loving son would his own mother.

"You know I did, but don't you dare eat it all at once or you will have a belly ache."

"Sure thing. I won't."

Confused about whether to offer her hand or reach out for an embrace, Angela stood awkwardly at the door.

Trevor apparently felt the same trepidation. "Uh, well, I do hope to see you again soon, Angela. I can see why you and Bella are such great friends and why the Davies family loves you so. You fit right in with them."

"They are the family I never had."

Trevor reached out and gently shook Angela's strong, yet feminine, hand momentarily while he held her gaze, curious about the thoughts that made her eyes sparkle the way they did. They parted in silence, as each turned inward to process the day.

9
___

Angela kept busy with helping Bella, joining the trail rides, snuggling Annie. On the second weekend of her stay, she went camping with Marco in the Black Hills.

"Auntie, don't you just love watching the sunset over the water?" Marco watched the horizon hanging above the bobber that was hovering offshore where the perch purportedly live.

"It is one of my favorite things because you get to see it twice, once right side up and once upside down. The colors are just fantastic."

"Yes, Grandma Vette says God is quite an artist."

"Your grandmother is a very wise woman. She loves her family and her community, and her God first. I am so happy that she is in your life…" Angela poked Marco in the ribs to lighten the conversation. "…and mi…"

"Woah, Ange, my bobber went under! And again!" Marco jumped up from the rock he was perched on and gave his pole a tug. "There, I think I hooked it."

"Great. Now, see if you can bring it through the wee… Dang Marco, look at your pole bend. I think you caught breakfast for tomorrow."

"Or maybe a midnight snack," he smiled as he held tightly on to the pulling rod. "I'm feeling a little hungry."

Marco reeled in an eight-inch perch, gently removed the hook with pliers, and tossed it into the bucket of fresh water. It was their first fish of the evening.

"I think if we could find his brother or sister, then maybe we could make a little meal." Angela wasn't a big fan of cooking and eating lake fish, but for Marco, she would do about anything. "I'm not much of a butcher. Do you know how to clean fish and cut them up?"

"Hey friends, how is it going?" A young father with two children had arrived for some nighttime fishing. Angela had met them as they set up camp near the campsite she and Marco chose. "Have you caught anything, or are you just fishing?"

"Hey there! Marco just caught our first. We were just going to flip the coin to see who would try to butcher it. Neither of us really knows how, and my phone isn't getting good enough service to watch a YouTube tutorial."

"Yeah, that's not going to help you out here." The stranger laughed and reached out a hand. "Hey, I'm Jason. These are my kids, Shelby, she's five, and Jackson, he's eight."

Angela shook the outstretched hand. "I'm Angela, and this is Marco."

"Tell you what. When you're done fishing, I'll help you fillet any fish you caught. I'm pretty good at it and Jackson's learning how to do it. It will be a good refresher for him."

"That would be terrific!" Angela was relieved to have a solution to their fish problem.

"Yeah, thanks man!" Marco put another worm on his hook and tossed the bobber back out onto the water.

"Okay, it's a deal. We're just going to go down the shore a ways there and see what we can catch. I had the kids out here a couple weeks ago and we each caught at least one. Seems this time of year is the best time to come out."

"Sounds good, Jason. Hopefully we will see you before too long."

As the family moved on, Marco turned to Angela. "Auntie, he seems like a nice guy, and he already has kids. Why don't you date him?"

Angela nearly choked on the water she was drinking. "He's probably married, Marco. I couldn't date a married man."

"Well, I don't think so. He doesn't have a wedding ring on."

"Are you kidding me? You checked him out? What's gotten into you, kid?" Angela reeled her line in to refresh the drowned worm.

"See, here's the thing, Auntie. If you find a man you love and get married, you could be here close to me and baby Annie, and of course Mom and Dad and Grandma Vette. I miss you so much when you're back at your place in New York, and Mom says you work too hard. You don't have enough fun. We could have lots of fun if you were here. I mean, like this. Isn't this fun?"

"Oh, Marco. It is so much fun here. I could move here, even without a husband. But I have a job that I really do love. And, of course, I couldn't go to Pilates or yoga class here."

"You could start Pilates and yoga classes here. I think that would be good for the ladies of Buffalo Ridge. They complain that they don't have enough to do and get fat in the winter when they're not out working cattle."

"Marco, you are the funniest kid I know. Do you sit around at the coffee gossip table downtown? Is that where you hear all this about the women?"

"No, mostly Grandma Vette tells Mom when they are working together at the café."

"I see." Angela smiled to herself, thinking of the conversation she would have with Bella about her gossipy son. She felt her fishing rod jerk slightly. "Hey, I think I have a bite."

"Wait a second before you reel it in. Watch to see if your

bobb…yup, it went under. Jerk back a pretty strong jerk to set the hook and reel it in. Fast, but not too fast."

"When did you get to be such an expert fisherman?"

"Grandpa Dan likes to take me fishing at the Spruce Dam a couple miles from the house. Like he says, sometimes we fish and sometimes we catch, but we always have fun."

"I like his outlook." Angela finished reeling the line in to find a tiny perch on the end.

Marco broke out in hearty laughter. "Auntie, I'm not sure that's even a fish. It looks like a fat stick."

"Thanks, buddy. I hope it's not hooked too deep. It will die an unnecessary death if I mess it up getting the hook out."

"That's something I'm really good at. Grandpa Dan says my hands are just the right size that I don't manhandle the fish. I'll get it out for you."

Angela watched as Marco gently manipulated the hook and lifted it out of the fish's mouth. Marco held the tiny fish out to Angela. "Do you want to throw it back?"

"No, that's fine, you can."

Marco slid the fish into the shallow water at the edge of the lake and gently moved his hand back and forth until the tiny fish swam away.

"I sure hope he makes it."

"He'll be fine, Auntie. We better hurry up and catch a keeper. It's getting dark out here."

Just as he finished speaking, his line bobbed again, and he reeled in another keeper. Angela looked over to see Jason busily taking a fish off Shelby's hook, while Jackson took a fish off his own.

"Your new friends seem to have found a school of fish over there. They are reeling them in right and left."

"We will be able to go see as soon as we pack up here. That's two keepers for us."

They gathered their gear and, using the flashlight on

Angela's phone, picked their way down the shore to meet up with Jason and his kids.

"Well, looks like you guys are doing a bang-up job catching over here." Angela looked in the bucket where four fish were moving around.

"Yeah, not too bad. This spot has been good to us, for sure." Jason finished adding a worm to Shelby's hook and tossed the line so the bobber hit the water just on the edge of the weeds.

"How about you guys? You catch your limit?"

"Considering our limit was two fish tonight, yes, we did."

"I caught them both. Auntie Ange caught one, but it was just a baby. We threw it back."

"No secrets with this kid around." Angela tussled the boy's hair. She was curious and glanced at Jason's left hand. Marco was right. No ring and no tan line.

"Right?! Kids tell it like it is. We've got enough now for breakfast, so I think we'll cash it in. You kids can keep fishing while I clean Angela and Marco's fish and then I'll do ours."

"Hey Marco, you want to just come down here with me and watch how I do this? Then next time, you can clean them for Angela."

Marco looked at Angela, who gave him an encouraging nod. "Yeah, thanks."

He followed Jason a few yards down the shore.

"Grab that clean water there, will ya? I've got the board and the knife all ready." Jason grabbed both fish buckets.

"Hey Jackson, are you catching on worms or do you use corn or something else?" Angela found something to talk about before the silence became awkward.

"We always use worms. Sometimes we dig them at Dad's house before we come and sometimes we buy 'em. Today we dug them because it was kinda late when Mom dropped us off."

Angela didn't inquire further, but it seemed clear that if

Jason and his wife weren't divorced, they were at least separated. Interestingly, she didn't generally look at every guy she met and wonder if they were single, or not. Angela had a long-standing belief, maybe from how she was raised, that if a man wanted to be in her life, whether as a friend or something else, he would be the one to make his wishes known. She had never developed a voice that let her pursue a man.

Just as she was losing herself in introspection, Shelby caught another fish.

"Hey, can someone help me?"

"Um, Angela, can you come hold my rod so I can help my sister?" Jackson motioned for Angela to step closer and take his fishing pole.

"Sure. What a nice big brother you are."

"I try. Sometimes I'm not that nice, but she likes me to help her." Jackson wrestled the nice-sized perch off the hook and carried it up to Jason. "That's enough now, Shelby. We're done fishing for tonight. I'll take this for Dad to clean. Miss Angela, will you please reel in my line?"

Angela was impressed with the young boy's take-charge attitude. Silently, she wondered if it's just him, his role as the eldest child, or his parents' circumstances that promoted that behavior in him. *Oh well, not mine to worry about*, she told herself.

THE TWO GROUPS walked back to the campground together. Jason built a small campfire and they sat around it as the kids tried to outdo one another with scary stories, none of which were very scary.

"Hey Shelby! That was a good campfire story, but if you want it to be scary, you need to change the punchline. A kangaroo-gone-berserk is probably not going to be found in the Black Hills of South Dakota. How about if it was a mountain lion instead? That could get really scary."

"Oh, thanks, Jason." Angela lifted one eyebrow, not sure whether to laugh or shake in fear. "Are there really mountain lions around here? Do I need to be worried they will come to our tent?"

"No. I mean yes, there are mountain lions here, but no, they really don't like being around people, so it's not likely they will bother you here."

Angela and Jason talked, mostly about the children, for about an hour. Angela found herself wanting to yawn and decided rather than embarrass herself, or Jason, she would wrangle Marco for bedtime.

"Jason, it's been awfully nice of you to let us hang out. I enjoyed talking. Just in case we don't see you in the morning, I'll say farewell now." Angela folded up her camping chair and Marco did the same.

"Hey, ya, it was nice to spend time with another adult. I'm sorry, all I did was talk about the kids. If you give me another chance sometime, I'll show you that I can hold my own in a conversation about other things, too."

Angela laughed. "I have no doubt that you can. I'm heading back to the east coast in a few days but give me your number and I'll let you know when I'm back in Buffalo Ridge. Maybe you could bring the kids out for a trail ride."

"Yeah Daddy, pleeeeeeze!"

"Shelby loves horses and the idea of riding, but she's never actually ridden. That would be cool, if it happens."

"The thing is, I only come out once or twice a year, so it could be a while."

"Okay. I'll give you my number. You can give me yours, and if I ever get to the east coast, I'll look you up. Or maybe just text you sometime."

"Sure. Sounds good." Angela typed in Jason's number and sent him her contact info. "There, you should have it. Now, Marco, let's get those chompers brushed and find our way into those cozy sleeping bags."

"Mr. Jason, it's been nice being at your fire. And thank you again for helping us with our fish. I guess since we didn't cook them tonight, we'll have them for breakfast. Good night, Jackson. Good night, Shelby. Have fun fishing tomorrow. We're going to go ride the zip line."

"You guys have a great time," Jason yelled as they walked away.

Angela and Marco turned and in unison responded, "You too."

10

———

"We met some cool kids and a guy that Auntie Ange kinda likes at the lake, and zip lining was soooo ahhhmazing! I want to do it again sometime and you can come with me." Marco was eager to share the adventures of the exciting weekend with his parents. "And then Auntie Ange bought me this really cool bolo tie to wear for school pictures and special occasions. It has a huge piece of turquoise and some gold on it."

Angela, gently rubbing Annie's back as she held her on her shoulder, smiled at Marco's storytelling.

"A guy? You're holding out on us Ange. Tell us…" Steve was curious as to how a guy became involved with Angela and Marco over a camping weekend.

"There's nothing to tell." Angela stopped rubbing Annie's back and point to Marco, "and you, young man, are making up stories."

"I am not."

"Did I say I liked Jason?"

"Jason, huh?" Bella was eager to hear Angela's side of the story.

"You said 'good night' in your sweet voice, and you gave him your number."

Angela's chest rocked with quiet laughter, trying not to disturb the sleeping infant in her arms.

"So that means I like him, huh? I'll have to remember that…and what's this about my sweet voice?"

"You know, the one that sounds like this." Marco's next line was in a higher-pitched tone with words flowing through smiling lips. "Good night, Jason, honey."

"There was no 'honey' that came out of this mouth little man."

"Okay, so you didn't say honey, but it was sweet talk."

Marco had the entire group laughing.

"Mom, can I go down to the stables and see if Clint needs help with the horses? I kinda missed them."

"Son, you were only gone two days!" Steve was inspired by the way Marco took to the ranch.

"I know, Dad, but that's a lot of time in horse years."

Again, the group laughed as they waved Marco out the door.

"He was good for you, then?" Bella was hopeful the two would have a great time together. Since the baby arrived, there had not been much time to focus just on Marco.

"He was great, and I think he enjoyed himself as much as I did."

"And did you really give Jason your number?"

"He asked, so yes, I did. I suggested that maybe when I come back to town the kids could come down and see the horses. His daughter, Shelby, loves horses, but the truth is I'll probably never hear from him again."

"I'll bet you do." Steve chimed in. "And another man I bet you'll hear from is Trevor. He seemed quite disappointed that you weren't in church yesterday."

"Ha! He would really be disappointed to learn that other

than visiting the chapel at the hospital on really rough days, I am rarely found inside a church."

"I'm not sure about that. That wouldn't really be his style. But he wanted to continue your conversation from Annie's baptism celebration. I hope you don't mind, but I did give him your number. He was asking me if you had every minute here planned before you leave, and of course I couldn't answer that."

"That's sweet. If I hear from him, I'll try to find some time to have coffee or something. Speaking of coffee, Bella, do you plan to go to coffee with the ladies in the morning? I want to do a little shopping before I go home, and I'll do it then if you're going in. Otherwise, I will find a time to go in myself."

"I do plan to go in tomorrow, and Yvette does, too. She said we could pick her up if we're going. She knows it's the last chance you will have this trip and the coffee crew would love to be able to see you before you leave."

"That's settled then. Can I help you at the café? Serve dinner or set up?"

"I think we're all set up, and of course you can help me. Steve's going to have Annie so I could use a little help. We don't have a huge crowd tonight, but they are a fun bunch! Every one of them went trail riding today and I'm sure there will pictures and stories shared. The entire group is connected through one friend or another. For fifteen years they have taken group trips and this is their first time to South Dakota."

"JEEEZUS SHERMAN, couldn't you make that horse stop shittin' today on the trail? Every time I looked, he was dropping them road apples," Bradley shouted to a large man in a Hawaiian print shirt across the room. The guests laughed and chattered more loudly than before. Each table was on their third bottle of wine and had swapped similar jabs all evening.

Angela was clearing dinner dishes from the guests' tables, preparing to serve dessert. "Is it going to be a problem for y'all if we serve Road Apple Pie?" The question was met with loud groans from the group.

"If I can please clarify, that's "Rushmore Road Apple Pie." Angela smiled brightly and flipped her long hair over a shoulder.

"It has rhubarb combined with apples. When I come around, just let me know if you would like cinnamon ice cream on your warm pie."

"Yeehaw! Sounds like a winner!" Craig from Chicago lifted his glass. "Compliments to the chef! The service and the food have been wonderful."

"Here, here," the crowd chimed in as they tipped their glasses, many draining theirs before pouring another.

"You weren't kidding! That was quite a lively bunch." Angela rinsed dishes and put them in the dishwashers while Bella scrubbed the pots and got organized for the following day.

"I think it's so wonderful what they are doing. They have made their own family of each other and have something to look forward to every year although Marci, that beautiful woman with the sparkly silver tank top on, said they have supported each other through loss of a child, two husbands and several parents during that time, but celebrated births and weddings, too." Bella was thumbing through her book of original recipes, looking for the flank steak marinade for the following day.

"It would be really nice to have friends like that. I have you out here, which I will never give up, but I would like to add to it, not necessarily for the adventure, at least initially, but because I miss you guys so much and I really don't have a group back home that are my peeps." Angela wiped her hands and took a drink from her wine glass. "I know, it's my fault, really, because I haven't made it a priority to develop a social life. I could give up my moonlighting job, but it keeps me busy and rent is so high."

"Have you thought about getting a new roommate to help pay for rent, instead of working that extra job?"

"I have, but not seriously. At first, it was emotionally so much easier to take that extra job to fill my time when you and Marco left." Angela dropped the dishtowel on the counter and rested her elbows on the counter's edge. "Honestly, I couldn't have thought of someone else living in your bedroom and sharing the apartment. I've stretched out into that space now and don't really want to share it with a roommate."

She stood up again and rested her hand on the towel. "You know what I think?"

"I think that you think there's a change blowing in for Angela Cavanaugh." Bella handed Angela a tray of clean glasses to put away.

"Just hearing you say that makes my stomach churn. I didn't realize until this trip just how stuck my life had become. I work, chat with my favorite barista while getting the same ole latte at the same coffee shop. I go to yoga class when I can fit it in and do the same routines without challenging myself or allowing myself a restorative class. I flirt with the same guy friends at work. It's safe, either because they are happily married, a decade younger, or gay."

"Well, at least you are keeping your skills up." Bella chuckled as they restocked the café.

"I wonder. Whatever skill I had, I developed in grade school when every little girl had a crush on Derek Malone, who was two grades ahead of me."

"Let me see that eyelash batting you do so well." Bella turned with narrowed eyes, waiting for Angela to perform.

Angela glanced sideways in Bella's direction, turned the

corners of her mouth upwards and blinked slowly, one, two, three times, mascara-coated eyelashes bouncing off her cheeks.

They laughed as Bella responded. "You really do need to work on that. It's almost creepy the way you looked at me sideways."

"Maybe you can give me some lessons. Whatever you did, you sure got a great man." Angela smoothed the tablecloth to set the table for the next morning's meal. "And speaking of the…"

"Ladies, how are you doing? It's getting pretty late, and I have one hungry baby here."

Bella glanced at her watch. "Oh, honey, I'm so sorry. We got lost in girl talk and now that I see her…" Bella looked down and pointed as milk began to leak from her breasts and stain her dress. "…I feel how long it's been. Poor baby. Has she been crying?"

"Actually no. I had enough milk in the fridge to last until she fell asleep about two hours ago. But knowing her schedule, I'm sure she's going to be happy to see you in 5…4…3…"

Bella took the sleeping baby from Steve and sat down. Annie stirred and rooted for her mother's nipple.

"Perfect timing honey. Thanks for bringing her down. How was Marco?"

"Great. He wants me to start training him on goat-tying. I set him up with a couple of YouTube videos so he could study the techniques. Then, he wanted to know if he could learn how to sew. Apparently, he saw someone in the video who had put colorful patches on their jeans, and he thought it was really cool."

"So, did you get out the sewing kit?"

Steve grinned and shook his head. "Naw. I told him grandma would teach him."

"She would love that!" Bella nodded and turned back to the beautiful baby snuggled at her breast.

11

———

"**I** hear you're getting ready to leave us again." Susan, the soft-spoken mother of Bella's sister-in-law, Kerry, joined them for coffee and to wish Angela well. "It was great you could come and be with Bella and the baby. You know, Yvette keeps me up to date on all the happenings."

Angela leaned her face in close to Susan's and lowered her voice. "Of course, she does. She's the best. But Susan, tell me what she says about me when I'm not around."

Susan laughed. "Really, all she has to say is that you're so beautiful, it's a shame you're single, and you work too much to have enough fun and a husband."

Angela laughed. "She says all that?"

"Well, you know, she is a pretty intuitive woman."

"Yes, I suppose she is." Angela grabbed her coffee cup and rose to refill it at the self-serve communal urn. "Would you like another cup, Susan?"

As she walked away from the table with the coffee cups, Angela thought about the repeated message she was getting about working too much. She was deep in thought when she heard her name called.

With a slightly desperate edge to his voice, Trevor called

her name again. "Angela! I was hoping to get to see you before you leave."

He held his hand out to take one of the cups. "Can I help?"

"Good morning. I've gotten pretty good at this waitress thing now that I've been helping out at the dude ranch. I'm good." She inched her way toward the coffee.

"Well, I was wondering…" Trevor's eyes darted, searching for something to focus on to calm his nerves. He grabbed a coffee cup and filled it for himself while Angela filled hers.

Angela turned away from the coffee urn and looked at Trevor, who had a tiny bit of his bottom lip pinched between his teeth. She grabbed the two full cups of coffee and slowly headed back to the table with Trevor right beside her.

"…um…is there any chance we could pick up our conversation before you leave? I realize there isn't much time left, but maybe if you aren't already booked tonight, we could have dinner, or…uh…" Trevor took a deep breath in, looked into Angela's eyes, and opened his mouth. Before another word came out, another patron stumbled, bumped his elbow, and coffee streamed down the front of his white polo shirt. "Yikes, that's hot!"

With his free hand, he reached out to steady a short broad-bodied woman who looked to be about eighty. "Ma'am, are you okay?"

She looked up apologetically. "I'm so sorry, sir. Oh, Pastor, it's you. I'm really sorry. I guess I fell off balance a little bit." In a frenzy, she grabbed a handful of napkins from the coffee cart and started daubing at Trevor's shirt.

"Oh Juniper, don't worry, it's fine. I've got another one just like this I can change into." Trevor took the napkins from Juniper and dunked them into his nearly empty coffee cup. He looked at her with genuine concern. "I haven't seen you for a while. Is everything all right?"

"Oh Pastor, I know it's been a while. My sister's been sick, and I've been taking care of her out there in Wyoming. She's on the mend now, so I'm back home. Just a bit tired, but happy to be back here."

"I'm sorry for your sister. It's great to hear she's getting better. It was generous of you to help h…"

"Hey, don't I know you?" Juniper squinted as she looked up at Angela, standing quietly beside Trevor. "Yes, I'm sure I do. Yup, that beautiful red hair and smile. You're that friend of Yvette's. No, that's not right. You're…um…Marco's momma's friend."

"Yes, Juniper, I'm Bella's friend."

"That's right, that's right. You stood up with Bella when they got married. Oh, my, she was a beautiful bride…and I just peeked at that babe of hers. She's a heartbreaker already. Ya know, she's just right over yonder with the coffee ladies."

The crowd was growing around the coffee cart and Trevor wanted to usher Angela out of the way and back to the table while squeezing in a moment to talk to her alone. "Thanks Juniper. We are going to take this coffee and go right over to her. We'll see you soon. You take care, now."

"Thank you," Angela said quietly to Trevor. "Susan's coffee is getting cold. Let me just take this to her and then let's step outside for a minute."

Trevor pointed in the direction of the front exit. "I'll just meet you out front. If I go over to that table, they will have me trapped for an hour."

"Sure. Meet you in a quick sec." Angela returned to the table with a quick explanation. "I'm sorry, Susan. There was a little accident at the coffee table, and it took some time to get back here. I apologize if your coffee got cold. If you'll excuse me for a minute, I just need to go talk to someone, then I'll be right back, I promise."

The old wood plank flooring had a thick, clear finish, helping Angela glide in her sandals to the exit. The heat of the day hit her in the face as she exited the cool, air-conditioned building.

"Hey, over here," Trevor called from a bench about ten feet on the right. "It's a little quieter here. I was trying, in my unusually ineloquent way, to let you know I enjoyed our last conversation and would like to continue it. I realize you don't…"

"Tonight, at seven? Join us for dinner at the dude ranch café?" *Gawd, Angela, do you always have to be in charge?* "Sorry. That's just like me, rushing the bus. Is that along the lines of what you were thinking?"

"Actually, better than I thought. I know you stay busy with the Davies family, and I was going to settle for a phone call from the airport lounge if that's all you had available." Trevor looked down at his coffee-stained shirt. "I accept and will be sure to have a clean shirt on when I see you again."

"Perfect. It's a da…dinner, then." Angela smiled and stood to leave. "I really do need to get back to say goodbye to the coffee ladies, since I won't be able to see them in the morning. They are such a fun bunch of women."

"They truly are. Thank you, Angela. I look forward to seeing you tonight."

"With your clean shirt." Angela turned to leave as Trevor stood. Her hand brushed his as she turned. Panic rose from her belly to her throat. *Is it okay to touch a preacher in public?* She walked on, as if she didn't feel the brush and had no visceral reaction to it.

The ladies at the coffee table welcomed her back and conversation picked up again. She answered a litany of questions about when she would be back, what she looked forward to in Manhattan, what was new with her job. Happy with the distraction, she cheerily answered each question.

"It's hard to say for sure when I will be back, but I think it will be sooner rather than later. This little princess is going to grow fast, and I don't want to miss it."

"Bella, I did something, and I hope it doesn't upset you."

Bella lifted her foot off the accelerator. Gravel roads still caused some anxiety and it sounded as if her friend needed an audience.

"Did you buy a third pair of boots? What could you possibly do that would upset me?"

"If it was only that easy. No, I bumped into Trevor, well, actually Juniper bumped into him when I was standing there. Anyway, I invited him out to the dude ranch for dinner."

The car was now at a standstill on the side of the road. "You what?"

"Oh, Bella. Is that bad? Do you have enough food? I didn't really think it through, I just was so nerv…"

"It's the most wonderful thing I could think of! He is such a good guy and not in your typical cowboy way. He has cowboy in his blood, but he also has big city experience and, well, a whole lot of life experience I'm sure he will share with you. Ange, it's good. No, it's great! How did it feel asking him?"

"Well, I pretty much rushed through it and hurried to leave. I had to put my charge nurse hat on. I'm just not that comfortable with one-on-ones with men. But, and you might think this is really weird, I accidentally touched him. I mean, we touched each other, by accident, and, well, is it sinful to touch a preacher in public?" Angela inhaled deeply. She didn't know what confession felt like, but she imagined it may feel like this, where you just dump the bad stuff on the table and run.

Bella, with raised eyebrows, dropped her jaw and threw her hand over her mouth. "You…touched…him?!"

Angela sank into her car seat and turned to look out the window. Her eyes stung.

"Ange…" Bella rested her hand on Angela's, trying to calm her. "I'm seriously kidding. It's no big deal. He hugs people in public all the time. Don't worry about it, I'm sure it's no sin."

"Well, the way I felt when he accidentally touched me may be sinful." Angela felt heat rise in her face.

"I guess you could always ask him. Instead, I suggest you just be your usual fun and cheery self and have a great evening. Of course, there is enough food. And I'm thrilled to have him join us. When he first moved back to town, we had him out, but it's been quite a while since he joined us."

Dinner was fantastic, as usual. Angela helped serve the guests and pour the wine so there was little time to visit with Trevor, who seemed to enjoy visiting with the dude ranch guests.

She had just finished eating when she felt a small hand on her shoulder. "Auntie Ange, Mom wants to see you in the kitchen."

"Sure. Please excuse me." Angela turned to Trevor and mouthed, "Sorry".

"No worries," he whispered back.

Bella was in the office feeding the baby. Steve was in the kitchen washing dishes.

"Ange, hun, why don't you and Trevor hang out up at the house? It's a nice night to be on the deck. We're going to be here for a while, and if you stay down here, I know you'll just work or entertain the guests."

"No, it's okay. We can help you." Angela was hesitant to be alone with Trevor. This was why she avoided dating - this out-of-place feeling where she couldn't control how she felt. It just happened.

"Angela, that's not an option. Listen to me. You are leaving in the morning and this guy wants to get to know you. I think you want that, too. Just relax and enjoy yourself. Really. It will be worth it. Set all expectations and fears aside and go with the flow. Here." Bella poured a short shot of spirits and handed it to Angela. "Drink this, fast, and march right out there and take that beautiful man up the hill."

Angela drank it down, wiped her mouth with the back of her hand, kissed the top of Annie's head, and waved to Bella as she backed out of the office.

<hr>

After chatting about the weather and other non-consequential things, Angela, on the offensive, asked the first really personal question. "Tell me more about your time on the east coast."

"That's a very big question for me. I'll give you the Cliff Notes version tonight and hopefully, we can chat again another day and I'll fill in the details." Trevor was buying time to avoid bleeding his childhood, traumas and all, all over this sweet night. He didn't want to turn this beautiful, smart, funny, caring, woman off so early. "I was born in New York, well, Astoria, to be specific. I lived with my mom there and around the Bronx, but ultimately, we ended up homeless. She was a dancer and that's a very competitive industry. She danced on Broadway for a while, but she had an injury that took her off the stage and when she healed, she just couldn't get through the auditions anymore."

"So, when did you come here to live with your grandparents?" Angela was accustomed to taking histories from patients and was a skilled inquisitor, but she was trying to make this more personal while not scaring him away. Left with a series of questions in her head about his early life in New York, she decided to shelve them in her memory for later.

"I was eleven, almost twelve, when I came here. Grams and Gramps had both suffered some health problems and needed help. By that time, theirs was a pretty small operation, but Grams still had chickens and sold eggs. Gramps raised a few cows and sold them for butchering. I learned to put up hay and spent a lot of time caring for the garden. I got to ride the horses, which was a real highlight for me."

"So, how was it going to school here compared to the city?" Angela knew she was monopolizing the conversation with her questions.

"I'm happy to answer that, but first, I get to ask you a question."

Angela took a deep breath. "Uh…okay, but be gentle."

Trevor shifted in his chair and took a long drink of his soda before asking the question that had been on his mind since meeting Angela. "How is a such a fantastic woman as yourself still single?"

Angela had been asked that question before, and her standard answer seemed inadequate now. "I don't think I can really answer that question. I mean, why has nobody asked me to marry them? That's really what it boils down to. Seems like you would have to ask them."

Trevor's eyes twinkled and his smile brightened. "Okay, give me their names and I'll ask."

"That's kind of the problem. There is nobody to ask. I don't really put myself out there to date anyone. I think I'm intimidated by the process of meeting men. I enjoy the life I have, for the most part, and haven't really looked to complicate it."

"Complicate it?"

"Well, I guess maybe it's how I grew up. My parents didn't really have a partnership, other than a financial one, that complemented the other person. They both were driven by their careers and didn't really express love and caring, at least not in front of me. Sometimes I think I must have been the product of their one careless night."

Angela looked away, thinking about what she had said and fearful that she had just tarnished their night.

"That's gotta hurt, to feel like you weren't an enhancement to an already loving relationship. Truth is, that happens more than you might know." Trevor allowed the silence. The words floated through the air. Eventually he asked, "Can I have a follow-up question?"

"Sure, I guess." Angela was still processing what she had said, but feeling supported by Trevor's calm reassurance.

"Would you be interested in creating something different than what you believe your parents had?"

Angela sat quietly, measuring her response. "That's a powerhouse question and my answer may change with time and experience. Today, I would say, I think so. But it sounds like a lot of work."

"Yeah, from what I've seen in others, it does require time and attention. However, with the right person it can be so worth it."

"I'll keep that in mind. Honestly, I think I need to sort this question out some more. I don't really have great role models. Bella and Steve might be the only exception. I mean, I've known couples that are happy or have been together for a long time, but most of what I know about relationships, other than my parents, are water cooler conversations where one partner is complaining about the other. Those who aren't complaining aren't saying anything, so I don't know if it's better or worse for them."

"I do think that's a problem. There aren't many role models. My parents never married. In fact, I really don't know that much about my father. My grandparents seemed happy, but they were a different generation and they stayed together and made it work for lots of different reasons. I don't have the answers, but I do have hope that it can be accomplished."

After a long silence, with both Angela and Trevor lost in thoughts of their own past experiences, hopes, and dreams, Angela saw the small shadow of a boy running up the driveway.

"Hey Marco. How are you, buddy?"

"Great, Auntie. Mom says I get to stay up late tonight since it's your last night here. What are you guys doing?"

"We are staring at the stars at the moment." Trevor waved his arm to the heavens. "I just love how they twinkle, like they are winking at us from above."

"Yeah, they're cool. Did you see the Big Dipper?" Marco had been using Angela's phone app to learn about constellations.

"I did, and Orion, the North Star, and Libra."

"Wow, you really know your stars. Maybe sometime you could teach me more. Auntie Ange is going to take her phone and then I won't get to study until she comes back."

"Of course. I will share what I know. I bet your mom or dad could also put the app on their phones and let you use that. But for tonight, can I show you Libra?"

"Yeah, sure."

"You see the Big Dipper?"

"Yeah."

"Follow the handle down and find the bright star below the handle." Trevor pointed while Marco studied the stars. "Do you see that bright star?"

"Yeah, I think I got it."

"Imagine that it is the top point on a diamond. There are four points in the diamond. Do you see them?"

Marco traced the stars with his finger. "I do. I see a diamond with the brightest star on top."

"Good. Now, on the left side there is another star. Find the star of the diamond that is below the top star and then trace your finger out to the left to find one more star. It almost looks like a kite with a tail coming out the side of it."

"Yes! I see it! That's amazing! Thanks, Trevor. That's so cool." Marco noticed movement on the edge of the deck. "Hey Mom! Trevor just taught me how to find the Libra constellation. Isn't that cool?"

"It sure is," Bella whispered as she carried the sleeping Annie up the deck stairs. "That is super cool."

BELLA AND STEVE gave a brief recap of their night to Angela and Trevor, before sending Marco to bed and excusing themselves. "We're beat, and tomorrow comes early. We need to leave by 8:30 to get you to the airport on time in the morning."

"Hey, I have time tomorrow. I have a meeting in the city, so I could take Angela to the airport, if you want." Trevor actually did not have an official meeting in Rapid City, but he really wasn't lying. There were parishioners he could visit at the hospice house and the hospital. *It might be a little lie,* he pondered, *but this woman may be my destined partner. Please forgive me.* Trevor was navigating a potential love interest for the first time since being ordained. Parts of it were still a mystery to him, but there was no mystery in the way he felt about Angela.

12

---

revor loaded Angela's luggage into the back seat of his crew cab pickup promptly at 8:30 the next morning and climbed into the driver's seat. "Thanks for letting me drive you this morning."

"I kinda didn't have a choice now, did I?" Angela stepped up into the front seat, trying to keep the short dress from creeping up too much as her long legs stretched out.

"I guess that's almost true. I have every confidence that if you didn't want me to be your chauffer, you would have protested. You didn't protest even a tiny bit."

"Truth, right there. I stayed out of that conversation." Angela untucked her hair from between the seatbelt and her shoulder.

Trevor backed the pickup out as Angela waived and threw kisses out the open window to her favorite people in the whole world. "Love you to the moon and back!" she called out. "Hold these kisses until next time."

"They are the greatest." Angela spoke quietly, as she choked down the emotion of leaving these dear friends. "I've always loved the Davies family and to see Steve so happy after he lost his first wife really brings great joy."

She glanced over as Trevor spoke, his perfect teeth bright white against darker skin, his blue eyes dancing as he looked at her.

"You sure do look great this morning, especially for being up so late." Trevor felt an ease with Angela and hoped he didn't come off as sounding too fresh. He kept his eyes fixed on the road to stop them from wandering over those red curls, short sundress, and long legs. "I'm sorry I talked your ear off so long last night. I probably should have left when Bella and Steve got home, but you're just such a great listener."

"Thanks. I've been told that before. I do prefer the listening part to the talking part. It's not that I mind sharing about myself. I'm kind of an open book for anyone who really wants to know me. It's just that I don't like small talk and I have a huge fear of oversharing."

Angela genuinely enjoyed listening to Trevor, although she didn't learn much about his life in New York or his mom and dad. A list of questions to ask him was taking up real estate in her thoughts. She even jotted some down in her journal last night, so she wouldn't forget.

"I kinda got that you don't like the small talk thing." Trevor negotiated the gravel road like a pro. "So, if I ask you questions, you can't possibly be at risk for oversharing. What do you think?"

"I'm not sure I'm exactly aligned with that, but it's probably more true than not." Angela offered Trevor one of the bottles of water she brought for the drive. "Ask away. It seems like there's something on your mind."

"There are lots of things on my mind this morning, most of which pertain to you. I was thinking more about what you said about why you're single, and I realized, one, I made the assumption that you were, and two, I assumed also that you date. Are you seeing anyone?"

"Oh, Trevor. I would not have accepted a ride to the airport with you, or spent hours chatting with you, if I was in a committed relationship with someone else. I just don't mix it up that way."

"That's a relief."

"As for dating, I don't do much. I have been set up before by friends, but my longest dating history is about six months and at that time we both agreed that we didn't feel like a long-term fit for each other. We talk occasionally, but there's nothing romantic between us."

Angela paused briefly before asking one of the questions on her list. She had asked Bella if she knew whether Trevor dated or not. Bella said that if he did, it wasn't anyone local. "So how about you? Do you date?"

"Oh. That's something that's changed for me over time. I dated in high school and college. I dated for fun. I wasn't looking for anything serious. Unfortunately, some of the women were, and I caused some hurt, unintentionally. When I decided to enter the seminary, I stopped dating and haven't dated since. That's been six years now."

"That must have been hard, going from recreational dating to none. Weren't you ever tempted to date during that time?"

"Of course. I am a man like any other. I knew it was an area of my life that needed pruning so I could eventually become the type of husband my future wife deserves. That meant I needed to stay focused on my personal development, and I couldn't do that while allowing play time that distracted me." They sat in silence briefly before Trevor added, "I hope that makes sense."

"It's your story. It doesn't have to make sense to anyone else, but I do think I understand what you're saying."

Now Trevor was curious. "So, would you consider your dating to be 'recreational' as you say, or purposeful?"

"Now you're getting into the tough stuff and possibly my greatest weakness. I fall fast and hard, and it has never turned out well for me. It's easier for me to avoid dating than to constantly control my expectations that the man is dating nonrecreationally, like I do. I'm not a one-night stand kind of girl. It's just not me, and lots of guys don't understand that. So, I've decided to continue to be someone I enjoy spending time with, and if I'm meant to be with someone whose ideals are aligned with mine, we will find each other. I can't play the casual dating game. It's just not me."

"That's really good to know."

Angela watched the landscape as they moved along the interstate, spotting cattle in the distance and following the small rolling hills recently sheared of their crops. It was a rare day with no wind.

"On a lighter note," Trevor continued, "what things do you do for fun when you're not working?"

"F-U-N-N, the four-letter word that has become my nemesis. So many of my friends have fun doing long nights of drinking and clubbing, eating elephant ears at the fair or snow cones on the boardwalk. Because I enjoy my work so much, I really need to be away for a few days before I can relax enough to start having fun. So, these two-week trips to see Bella and the gang are my idea of fun." Bella paused to watch as a car sped by them, then weaved in and out of traffic ahead.

Trevor checked his mirrors to see if there was a high-speed chase. With a wrinkled forehead, his eyes no longer danced in the sunlight of the morning. "That's so careless, driving like that on this busy road where most of the travelers are tourists and aren't familiar with where they are going."

"Yes, that's an accident waiting to happen right there. It's that kind of foolishness that puts people in my ER, if they survive that long."

After a few moments of silence, Trevor patted his left breast pocket gently and said quietly, "That made my heart race, and it's not a good feeling."

"It should. That was terribly reckle…" Angela paused to take in the scene ahead. Cars and pickups were pulling off on both shoulders of the road, and people were getting out of their vehicles. "Trevor, slow down! I think there's an accident."

Trevor had noticed the changes in the traffic pattern and was already slowing down. "Angela, I think we need to stop."

"Yes, yes, stop, please!" Angela's emergency room nurse instincts took over, even after a two-week break. "I need to help if I can."

They scanned the area causing the havoc. Trevor pointed in front of Angela. "There - down in the ditch, up against that cement culvert."

"Oh, what a day to wear cute sandals and a dress! I'm going to go down there and check on the driver and any passengers. Will you see if there's another car up here and check them out, too? This doesn't look good."

Trevor grabbed a dress shirt hanging from the back seat of his truck and handed it to Angela. "OK. Here, throw this over your dress. Want me to find you some other shoes in your suitcase? There might be rattlers down there."

"Great, one more thing to worry about. Yeah, thanks for the shirt. There's a pair of short boots in my small duffel. If you get a chance, send them down with someone. Here I go. Nurse Ange to the rescue."

She bounded out the door and raced down into the ditch toward the SUV lying on its side against the concrete culvert with two wheels suspended in the air, still spinning.

"Hey, lady," a man yelled up at her. "Be careful coming down here! This car is leaking gas. I can smell it."

"Thanks, I will be. I'm a nurse. Maybe I can help."

"Great! I'm an EMT from the next town over. I've called emergency services. They should be here soon, although it's a volunteer service, so it may take them a bit."

Half gliding and half running, Angela made it to the upturned car. She heard a child's voice pleading for help and calling out, "Mommy!"

"I hear a child. You check the back seat. I'm going to the driver," Angela directed the EMT.

She quickly assessed the unconscious woman in the front seat. The left side and front of her head were bloody from gashes. She grabbed a piece of clothing lying on the car seat next to the driver and quickly put pressure on the bleeding wounds while she continued to assess.

"Hello. My name is Angela. I am a nurse. If you can hear me, open your eyes." There was no response. Looking down the body, she saw that the woman was obviously pregnant, but did not appear to be at term yet. The dash was pushed into her lower legs and the steering wheel was resting just above the pregnant belly. A seatbelt burn was already apparent on her neck, and as Angela unbuckled the belt and unbuttoned her shirt, she could see redness across her chest.

The EMT leaned into the back of the upturned car to assess the boy in a car seat. "Nurse, this is Phillip, he is five years old. He and his mommy were on their way to see the doctor for her checkup today."

"Hi, Phillip. It's nice to meet you. My name is Angela. How are you feeling?"

"My tummy hurts really bad."

"There's one of those plastic lap trays he was watching an iPad on. Looks like the front seat came back and shoved that tray into him. His pulse is strong right now at 110. He has a red mark across his abdomen just below the area of the diaphragm."

"EMT - what is your name?"

"I'm Evan, ma'am."

"Evan, as soon as I can, I'm going to try to reach over and see if I can't get that seat to move up and unwedge that tray, but right now the car is too unstable for me to crawl in deeper. We'll have to wait for emergency crews to help. Sounds like he might have rib involvement and maybe a bleed. Watch his breathing closely and look for vomiting, changes in mentation, skin color, and temperature. Get your people on the phone if you can and give them an update so they are prepared."

"Phillip, is your mommy going to have a baby?"

"Yes. A baby girl. We call her pumpkin because she's a Halloween baby. That's what daddy says."

"You're a smart boy. Thank you for all that information."

As Angela talked to Phillip, she rubbed the woman's sternum hard with her knuckles.

"Phillip, what's your mommy's name?"

"Suzanna. Daddy and Grandma call her Susie or Suze. I just call her mommy."

Still rubbing Suzanna's sternum, Angela called to the woman to open her eyes.

"Suzanna. Suzanna. My name is Angela. Can you open your eyes, please? Open your eyes."

Angela observed fluttering of the woman's eyelids. Suzanna started to move her head as she awakened.

"Suzanna. You've been in an accident. I need you to hold still. Don't try to move."

"Hey, nurse, here's some boots for you."

Angela didn't turn around to talk to the person, but responded. "Thanks. Now can you find me some clean rags or something to hold against these bleeding wounds? Drop the boots anywhere and go back and ask anyone up there for gauze or clean rags or something. Hurry, please!"

Angela asked, "Suzanna, where do you hurt?"

A shaky, panicked voice called out. "Phillip, where's Phillip?"

"Here, Mommy. I'm ok, but my tummy hurts."

Angela continued to assess Suzanna, now that she was conscious, and her breathing seemed stable. Her pulse was high, and Angela was concerned about bleeding. She touched Suzanna's arm. "Can you feel my hand on your arm, Suzanna?"

"Mm hmm."

"How about now, can you feel my hand on your thigh?"

"I don't feel my legs at all. What's happening? My baby! Is my baby okay?"

"I need you to stay calm, Suzanna. We have an ambulance on the way."

"That car. It cut right in front of me. I had to swerve to miss it."

"Suzanna, we need to just focus on you right now. There are a bunch of witnesses that I'm sure the police will talk to. I need to reach in to feel your legs. I'm going to be gentle so the car doesn't rock. I need you to keep your head absolutely still while I do this. You let me know if you feel any pain, okay?"

"Okay."

Angela reached in deep under the crushed dash to find Suzanna's lower legs. Her gloveless hands felt the warmth of fresh blood. "Evan, I've got a gash involving the popliteal of the right leg. I can barely reach it, but I'm going to need to put pressure on it."

She quickly took Trevor's shirt off and held it tightly against the pulsating wound. She listened for sirens, but heard nothing yet. "How far out is the ambulance?"

<hr>

"The ambulance is eleven miles away, and the other emergency vehicles are right ahead of them."

Trevor appeared beside her. "Angela, hey, anything I can do to help?"

"This is going to sound weird, but I need to get a little deeper into the car without tipping it. I think if I could stand on somethi…"

Trevor knelt with his right foot on the ground. Patting his thigh, he offered the footstool for Angela to stand on. "Here."

"Thanks. If you see the car move, get out of the way. I'll be okay." Angela kicked off her sandals and stepped up onto

Trevor's leg. "First I'm going to try to reach over and pull the passenger's seat up. Evan, you ready?"

"Yes, we're good. Phillip is stable."

Angela reached in as far as she could and grabbed the bar to release the seat. It slid forward quickly.

"Evan, watch him closely. That pressure may have been controlling internal bleeding."

"Yes, ma'am. Stable for now. Keep talking to me Phillip. Tell me some more about your puppy, Puds. You said he liked to swim?" Talking continued in the back seat while Evan monitored the young boy.

"Okay. Now, I'm going to need some more something - gauze or cloth, anything for this bleeding."

Angela reached out as a good Samaritan handed her a clean towel. "Here. Some guy had it in his gym bag. He said it was clean."

"Thanks, I sure appreciate this." The towel quickly disappeared from sight as Angela stuffed it against Suzanna's leg deep under the wreckage that once was the dash. "Suzanna, you still with me?"

"Mm hmm." Suzanna's eyes were closed, but she was still responsive.

Finally, the wail of a siren came through, gradually becoming louder. "Sounds like help is here. You still doing okay back there Evan?"

"Holding our own, here," Evan answered.

"Phil, you're okay baby?"

"Mmm...yeah, Mom." Phillip's arms were wrapped around his middle and his face was pale and long.

Hearing rustling in the tall grass of the ditch, Angela turned to see paramedics and firemen scurrying toward the car.

"Hey, Evan. Hello, ma'am. I'm Captain Matthews with the paramedics."

"She's a nurse," Evan answered the Captain's questioning glance.

Angela sighed with relief. "Good to see you guys. In the front here I have Suzanna Parker, 35-year-old Caucasian, 6 months pregnant. Initially unresponsive, but responded within minutes to sternal rub. Pulse has been ranging between 90 and 120. She has a large gash on her right lower leg and pulsating blood loss suspicious for popliteal artery injury. She has no sensory perception below the beltline."

Captain Matthews observed carefully as Angela continued to give a thorough assessment of Suzanna and Phillip.

"Thank you, ma'am! I see you've given them excellent care here in the field. Parks and Johnson, get this car stabilized. Martin, get in there and keep compression on the driver's leg while…I'm sorry, I didn't get your name."

"Angela, Angela Cavanaugh. I'm an ER nurse."

"…while Ms. Cavanaugh backs out of there. I'm sure the police will want to ask you some questions. Mrs. Parker, nurse Cavanaugh is going to slowly back out now…"

Suzanna opened her eyes and, while keeping her head still, turned them toward Angela. "Thank you, Angela, you are our angel."

"You are most welcome, Suzanna. You and Pumpkin and Phillip are going into capable hands. They'll get you to the hospital for further assessment."

Angela stabilized herself with a hand on Trevor's shoulder while she quickly slipped her sandals back on. She paused briefly by the backseat. "Phillip, what an amazing brave young man you are! Thank you so much for helping us out."

She reached out to pat Evan's arm. "Great job Evan. Thanks for being here."

"You're welcome," he responded, without taking his eyes off his patient.

"I have to check in with the police, Trevor. Did you already talk to them?" Angela looked to Trevor who walked beside her as they headed up out of the ditch. "Hey, are you okay? You look a little pale."

Trevor paused and took Angela's hand, caked with remnants of dried blood. "I will be fine, but wow, you are amazing. The way you took charge and all those details you were able to give that Captain. I mean…I've seen it on T.V. before, but never a live version. You saved that woman. I can feel it in my gut and…well, I admit I am a bit woozy from all that blood, but I'm wowed by you, Angela."

"Uh…thanks." Angela dropped her hand from Trevor's, feeling contaminated from the accident scene and not wanting to contaminate him. "That's kinda what my days look like in the ER, on the exciting ones, when it's not all just vomit and diarrhea."

"Buzz kill, right there."

"Sorry, just being real. But I have to admit that this was intense and even I am a bit shaken. I'm glad you were there to help. It made a difference for me." She looked down at herself and then blankly around the accident scene. "I really need a shower, so if we can find the investigating officer…I'm sure I missed my plane. I'll need to figure that out. But I've got to find a place to shower."

"I've got an idea. Let's find Officer Shank. He had several eyewitnesses he was interviewing. You can talk to him while I phone a friend."

13

"Are you sure it's okay to stay at the parsonage with your friends? I mean, I don't want it to look like you're..."

"Angela, it's okay. They have two extra bedrooms, in separate wings of the house, and my friends are cool. James was one of my mentors when I was searching for my life's direction and Shelly was part of my support, too. They once were in Buffalo Ridge, back in the day."

"I'm just kinda weirded out about how to act around a pastor. We've never really talked about my religious upbringing and, well, failures in that department."

"There's plenty of time for that. I'm still coming down off the excitement of this morning's events. Seriously, how do you live with all that adrenaline day-in and day-out, without burning out?"

Angela broke her gaze from staring out over the lake in the middle of the city. Trevor had brought her here for a quiet picnic dinner. "Before we go there, can you show me what's in that bag of stuff you brought? I am suddenly starving. I'm not avoiding the question, honestly, I just realized that I haven't eaten since...well, I guess last night, and even then, I was too busy and anxious to really sit down and enjoy it."

"By all means, let's get you fed. Shelly knows this little catering place they use sometimes. She's friends with the owners. She called them and they put something together, so honestly, I'm not even sure what all we have. I do know that she made us a thermos of white tea, with rosehips. She said it's a great relaxant. I thought it couldn't hurt."

"You are so right. It's been a pretty big day, and I have a feeling it isn't over yet."

Trevor looked up from unpacking the food, smiled sweetly, and braced himself against the urge to lean in and kiss her tenderly.

<hr>

THEY ATE in comfortable silence and small talk. Angela patted her flat stomach. "Compliments to the chef. That was the finest and most welcomed assortment of wonderful food I have had since…well, any meal at Bella's actually, but nonetheless, it was a beautiful picnic. That risotto was top notch."

"What about those ribs and wings? I never would have guessed those would be available on the fly like this."

"Also, very tasty and a real treat. You know, I look around me and all this day has brought, and I just feel like I, well, we've been in the right place at the right time all day."

"It is interesting, isn't it? How the day unfolded?"

"I know, you're going to say it's all divine intervention…"

"Am I?" Trevor was quick to question this.

"Well, isn't it your job to say something like that?"

"Do you think it is, Angela? Divine intervention?"

"Honestly, maybe. I really only know that phrase by going with a dear friend to Alcoholics Anonymous. A neighbor in my complex. He came knocking on my door in the middle of the night, not long before Bella and Marco moved in with me, so it's been several years. He was vomiting blood." Angela paused to check on Trevor. "Sorry, that may not be the best imagery right now."

Trevor waived her worries away with his hand. "It's fine. I'm fine."

"I got him to the hospital and sat with him while they got the bleeding stopped and transfused him. He poured his heart out to me about the death of his partner, pressures at work, being estranged from his family, and other things. He confessed that he was a functional alcohol for quite a while, but had been hitting the bottle hard for months."

"My heart goes out to anyone in that much pain."

"Yes, mine too. He wanted help to stop drinking. He was really scared by what he was going through. I agreed to help him by going to AA meetings with him."

"That was quite a commitment considering your workload."

Angela nodded. "It was. Thank goodness you can find meetings around the clock in the city. Many times, we would go to a 3:00 a.m. meeting and then have breakfast before we both went to work, then met up after work for another meeting and dinner. The trade-off was that I got him to go to my yoga class with me."

She paused and smiled with the memory of those days.

"How is he now? Your friend...?"

"Robert. He's doing really well, and next to Bella, he is my best friend, along with his lovely new partner Alecia. He has stayed sober and is still in counseling. He reconciled with his mother. Sadly, his father passed away shortly after Robert worked on Step Nine and made amends with his parents. He invited me on that journey."

"He really trusted you."

"Yes, he did. It was the hardest of all the steps for him. He just felt like he had failed them so many times; he couldn't bear the thought of looking at the sadness in their eyes. The reunion was so touching, and of course they had missed their son all those years he avoided them."

Angela pointed toward the north sky, which was just beginning to darken. "Look, the first star is out."

"Time to make a wish."

After scanning the sky and silently making a wish, Trevor looked back to Angela. "Divine intervention?"

"So, what I understand from AA is that when God, or the Universe, Higher Power, or whatever, conspires to bring the alcoholic and help together, that is divine intervention."

"I think that's what happened today, and of course, I can't name the source for anyone else, but in my eyes, it was God that made that happen."

"I bet you do. It might be. I can't speak for Suzanna or Phillip. For me, I get more comfort by not naming the source, being open to options."

"Okay."

"Okay? That's it?" Angela was surprised. "I mean, isn't it your job to convince me otherwise?"

"It's my job to be available to show you what I believe and why, to be available to you when and if you want to talk about your beliefs, and to love all people, yourself included. You see, Angela, I see you and your beautiful soul. You treat people with dignity and respect. You do good in the world. You are the epitome of what Jesus wants us to do. How could I ever fault you for not using his name, but walking the path he desires for us?"

"Somehow, I think this part of the conversation is not over, but for now, can we talk about something less, um, controversial?"

"Of course. How about those White Sox?"

Angela laughed. "Now you're talking controversy."

"Okay, maybe so. I've really enjoyed the time we've spent together. I know we really just met, but I feel a sense of a connection, you know, that type that you can't put into words, but you know it's there?"

Angela felt it too, but she had felt it before and there had been no happy ending. She couldn't bring herself to respond. There wasn't enough time, or, frankly, emotional space tonight to sully their good time with her old un-love story.

Sensing Angela's need to retreat and be still, Trevor started gathering the food containers. "I'm going to clean this up. Then, would you like to walk around the lake, at least partway? There are some swans over there that like to show off."

"I would love that. I'll get the blanket and the thermos. If the truck's locked, can you unlock it so I can put them away?"

"Yeah, sure."

Angela put her sandals back on. She wondered if the cute ones she had worn earlier in the day would ever come clean. They were soaking, along with her dress, back at the parsonage.

<hr>

"If we head south from here," Trevor pointed down the sidewalk to a viewing platform extending over the lake, "we should see the swans and ducks."

Angela looked down the pathway. It was dusk and the recently set sun was still showing off its colors, reflected on the horizon of the western sky. The moon was rising, and the reflection danced on the lake. As they approached the platform, Angela saw a series of gazebos spread out across the park, each lit up with garden lights. The idyllic scene brought a sense of nostalgia that she couldn't associate with any past experience. It felt...romantic, like a Hallmark movie.

"It's nice that they have the stairs lit up."

"Isn't it? Almost like they expected us." They shared a smile.

Trevor gently pressed his hand on Angela's elbow, ushering her to the rail. "See, down there."

He pointed out onto the water about twenty feet from where they stood. Two swans rested on the water, pale pink and peach, as the colors of the sunset created the watercolor backdrop for the heart shape suspended between the swans. Their long necks rose from where they were pressed together just above the water, each curving outward and then back inward as their beaks crossed in front, at the base of their heads. In that heart-shaped opening, Angela saw a cygnet watching the adult pair.

"The tea was nice, but this is the most relaxing moment I think I have ever enjoyed," Angela whispered to avoid disturbing the serene scene before them.

As she quietly observed, daring not to move, Trevor sneaked a step back and stealthily took the phone from his shirt pocket. Silently, he turned the camera on and pointed it toward Angela and the swans.

"Hey Angela," he said softly. As she turned, he caught her in a series of photos, with the swans in the background.

"Now, that was sneaky. If you have anything decent in that bunch, send me a copy, will you?"

"I will, gladly. I'm sure they will all be fantastic. How could they not?!"

"Oh, Trevor. What a perfect ending to a difficult day. I wonder how Suzanna and Phillip are doing."

"We could stop by the hospital on the way back. What time did you say your flight leaves tomorrow?"

"I should be at the airport at about eight in the morning."

"Then I think we have plenty of time to sneak in a quick visit at the hospital tonight. I'm sure they'll let us in to see them. It's close by. But before we leave this moment. I have to say something."

"Yeah?" Angela's heart was beating in her ears. She rubbed damp palms against her jeans. "What's that?"

"I would love to kiss you, and before you freak out, I won't. But I just need you to know that I really like you, Angela, and I don't think that's going to change the more I get to know you."

Angela could not form words. She smiled, then looked away from Trevor, back to the swans, who were now gliding along the top of the lake with a larger group. "I…I don't know what to say. I'm on foreign ground here. My heart is all in, but my fears and my questions are taking over my head."

"I get it, I do. I wouldn't know what to do with a guy like me either."

Angela turned back and placed a hand on Trevor's chest. "That's not it at all. It's me." She paused. "Would you settle for a hug?"

Trevor wrapped his arms around her, resting his cheek on the top of her head.

Being a few inches shorter than he, Angela's face rested comfortably along his neck, against his shoulder. She felt at peace for a long moment. Quiet infused her mind. Her heart calmed.

<hr>

"Thank you so much for bringing me by the hospital. I didn't think they would let us in." They sat in the truck, recapping their visit in the hospital parking lot.

"Me too. I have some contacts I could have used in the chaplain's program, but I'm glad it worked out."

"Suzanna's husband. He was so sweet." Angela had met many spouses and partners over the years working the ER and it was always comforting to know a patient had the support of a loved one.

"Phillip looked great, don't you think? I mean, I'm no medical professional, but he sure seemed to have a spark."

"He did, and he remembered us. I couldn't believe it. After

all that trauma and drama today, he remembered us and was happy to see us."

"So, will the doctors have to do anything more for him?"

"Right now, they are keeping a close eye on his blood levels. He may have a small tear in his spleen, so the doctors are watching him."

"What will they do for it?" Trevor knew cows and horses, but human medical conditions were still a mystery to him.

"If there is a small tear, it would be one that should eventually heal itself. If it was a major tear, they would have had to do emergency surgery right away."

"What was it her husband was saying about Suzanna and the baby? I'm not sure I caught it all in the medical jargon."

"They had to take her into surgery to repair the tear of the vessel in her leg. She lost a lot of blood and needed to be transfused but was stable. They are concerned about potential internal bleeding and possible concussion, so they are observing her closely in intensive care. So far, the pregnancy looks stable."

"Leon asked for contact information. I shared mine, and I can give it to you if you want it. He knows Suzanna will want to reach out and share her appreciation when she is on the mend."

"Oh, yes please. I will send him my contact info, or you can. I want to know when little 'Pumpkin' makes her way into the world. Suzanna will probably have to take it easy the rest of her pregnancy, but hopefully, all goes well."

"I think we should get you home to bed. You have a big day tomorrow."

"Oh, hey, weren't you supposed to go to a meeting today?" Angela remembered that Trevor was her designated driver to the airport originally because he needed to be in town for a meeting.

"It's okay. It was nothing, really." *Literally, nothing.* Trevor turned the key and drove back to James and Shelly's.

There was no sign of the couple when Angela and Trevor returned to the house. "Looks like they have retired for the night. I'll see you in the morning. I'm sure Shelly will want to give us coffee and breakfast in the morning. It'll be there if you want it."

"Okay. Thanks. Let me just see how my night goes. Thanks, Trevor. You were really wonderful today and I enjoyed our evening together. You know, I like you a lot, too." Angela turned down the hallway to her bedroom.

Content and excited, Trevor watched her walk away.

14

"No, wait. Tell me that part again, where you were with the swans."

Robert and his partner Alecia were thrilled to finally spend time with Angela after her return from South Dakota a couple weeks prior. They had all been busy, but finally found this Sunday evening to catch up over dinner.

"You know what? It's going to be easier just to show you." Angela opened her phone and showed them the pictures Trevor sent while she was in flight, returning to New York.

"Oh, sweetie, this picture alone could make me cry! Is it really that beautiful there? I mean, wow. And look at you! You look absolutely radiant here." Robert sensed a difference in his friend since her return, even though they had only texted, and bumped into each other once at the mailboxes.

"That picture is exactly how it looked that night, and thank you. I don't know that I felt especially radiant, more like a bundle of nerves wearing a smile. But that is exactly how the lake and the swans and everything looked. And here, if you could see it…" Angela pointed off the screen to her right, "there is a series of gazebos that are lit up with those hanging garden lights. I mean, it was just so…"

"Romantic, honey, that's what it was." Alecia handed the phone back to Angela. "So, what about the guy. Do you have any pictures of him?"

"No. I didn't get any."

"What?!" Robert and Alecia said in unison.

"But I pulled this one off the internet."

Angela flashed a photo of Trevor to her friends. He was dressed in jeans and a shirt, standing by a fencepost. It was part of some interview the local paper had done when he returned to the area.

Alecia snatched the phone out of Angela's hands. "Oh, hun, he's a hunk." She turned to Robert, "No offense babe."

"None taken. Let me see that." Robert studied the photo. "A real cowboy, there. He actually looks like a nice guy."

"He is a nice guy. But look…" Angela took her phone back and scrolled through photos Bella sent from the baptism. "Here he is at Annie's baptism."

"Where? Oh, my gawd!"

"What?!" Robert leaned toward Alecia to see the photo.

"Wait, he's the preacher?" Robert's entire bald head seemed to wrinkle in confusion.

"That's right. He's the preacher. Pastor Trevor."

"Um, I don't know what to say, Ange. That one caught me by surprise." Robert knew Angela wasn't particularly religious. She wasn't anti-religious either.

"Well, I figure if you can find a higher power at AA, maybe I can figure it out, too." Angela didn't really know what more to say. She wasn't sure where the relationship would go, if anywhere, and didn't know anything about dating a man of the cloth.

"You will, and if he is all that, like you say he is, it'll be worth the journey. I mean, look at me. Who would have thought an awesome guy like Robert would put up with my crap. I've got my own baggage, as you know."

"So, have you heard from him since you got back?"

"Only like every day. He knows I have a crazy schedule and stuff, so he'll send me a sweet or funny text a couple times a day and I have an open invitation to call or whatever. We did FaceTime the first weekend after I got back, and then last week we talked on the phone."

"So, what are you thinking? Is this guy a keeper?" Alecia looked at the photos again. "If you asked me, I would say yes, but then, you didn't, did you?"

"I've got a long way to go before I know that. I mean, there's the whole preacher thing, and I'm not religious. Then, the whole Jason thing, well…"

"Oh Ange. You can't let that creep steal your chances at love. He was no better than Marco's dad. He was never going to commit. He's not capable. I know you loved him. I know you did, but he didn't deserve you."

Angela felt her eyes brim with remnants of the past hurt but watched Robert as he spoke. She knew she needed to hear it.

"It's pretty easy to sit back and feel sorry for yourself for not getting what you thought was a possibility, a potential. I can see how you would fall for him. He showered you with attention and gifts and lord knows he's handsome and smart, and all that…"

"Robert, I'm not sure you're helping her."

"Yes, I think I am. He just loved himself and feared love too much. He's the kind of man that always needed a backdoor because he never wanted to be totally alone."

"A backdoor?" Angela wasn't sure she understood what Robert was talking about.

"Yeah. He always needed a woman he could go back to when his current fling failed, and it always did and will. A classic narcissist, I think. He would say he didn't want to hurt you but knew he would and did it anyway. Classic, I tell you.

It's like this: an alcoholic is addicted to alcohol, a user to drugs, right?"

Angela nodded. "That's my understanding."

"A narcissist is addicted to attention and if you give them that, you are their enabler. If you challenge the narcissist's quest for attention and self-importance, you threaten their addiction."

"That's what I did when I started talking about settling down and having a family with Jason, I guess."

"That's right, and that's when he moved to the next fling, or maybe she was an old one still willing to give him attention."

"I think I understand, but there's still a wound there."

Alecia jumped in. "That's because you're like me. You wear your heart on your sleeve and don't expect the guy to take advantage of you or kick you to the curb when you're being nice. I mean, I didn't meet that guy, but believe me, I had plenty of my own until I learned that there are plenty of people out there willing to take advantage of your sensitive soul. You have to learn to put on some armor, but then take it off when someone proves they are trustworthy. I think that this guy, this Trevor, I think he's worth you taking the armor off and opening your heart."

"I hear you. I do. I just don't know about the religion thing and how hard it would be to have a relationship, and if I would ever fit into a church." Angela thought a moment. "Or, where that church would be. I mean, I have never really considered leaving the city, and I don't even play the piano…or sing, for that matter." Angela paused to share a moment of levity; and her shoulders relaxed into their natural position.

"So, what does Bella think of all this?" the ever-curious Robert asked.

"I haven't really talked to Bella about this. We talk regularly, but I can't quite manage to bring this subject into the conversations. He's her minister, for gosh sakes! And a friend of the family. I hate to put her in an awkward position."

"Oh, so sorry, hun. Makes it more difficult when you can't talk about this with your best friend." Robert poured the remains of the wine into the women's glasses, and refilled his water glass. "I'm so glad we had this time together. There is so much for you to think about. I don't really know anyone dating or married to a holy man, but maybe you do? Could you talk to them?"

"There's a nurse at work whose sister is married to a Baptist pastor. I guess I could see what she knows."

"I think you might learn a lot from the preacher himself, if you would just talk to him about your concerns. They probably prepare them for that in school, or what is it they go to, not monastery but…?"

"Seminary, babe. They call them seminaries. Monasteries are for monks."

"Yeah, that's right. If he were a monk, we wouldn't be having this conversation, would we." The group chuckled.

"This has been a delightful, and grueling evening. Thank you both for having me over." Angela picked up her empty glass and took it to the sink.

"Can we please not wait so long to do it again?" Robert pleaded. "I think you're on the precipice, sweetie, of something big, and I want to witness it, kind of like you did for me when we went to all those meetings, and you played my wingman for Step 9. I love you like a sister and want to be there for you."

Angela reached out and hugged him. "I love you, my brother. I wouldn't change one thing about our friendship, really." She pulled back and moved to hug Alecia. "Thank you both for the beautiful evening. Sunday evenings are for us when we can make it work. I'll look at my schedule and let you know about next week. I'll shoot you a text. Are you two available?"

"Absolutely, hun, and you are welcome. You can also reach out when it's not Sunday. Hmmm, I think we may be onto something here. Ritual? Communion?"

Angela smiled at Alecia, and then at Robert. "You two are the best. Thank you again."

"Need help getting home?" They laughed and waved as Angela sauntered to the elevator, lost in thought and feeling hopeful.

15

"Oh, honey, that's a tough gig." Teressa talked over the unresponsive patient brought in from a local nursing home. "My sister, she tells me all the time how lucky I am that I didn't marry a preacher, like she did."

Angela swallowed hard. She had worked with Teressa - a fifty-something woman from South Carolina who followed her Brazil-born husband to New York - for years. "And I just tell her, there ain't no way I would marry me one of those uptight stage hogs wantin' all that attention."

"And you didn't. Richie is such a great guy. Hey, you guys singing in the club again sometime? I've got some friends I'd like to bring down." The duo sang at an employee after-party one Christmas and stunned the crowd.

"Sure are. We'll be at the Pink Flamingo the Saturday after next. Bring your friends and come down." Teressa continued to assess their patient. "Pass me that suction, will ya, girl."

The two worked to complete and document the patient's assessment before the doctor entered the bay. After the doctor left, as they were carrying out the orders, largely intended to keep the dying woman comfortable, Angela continued to probe. As far as she knew, Teressa was the only person she knew who might have some insights into married life with a preacher, albeit second-hand.

"So, back to your sister. Was she a religious woman when she met her husband?"

"Ha!" Teressa gave Angela a sideways look that could have shot her to the moon if it weren't for gravity. "Yeah, we went to church and sang in the choir, but I was the one sitting home on Saturday night with momma and pops while she was sneaking out and meetin' this boy or that one down by the river. That girl, mmmmm mmmmmm she was troubled. Drinkin' and smokin' and, I'm sure there was sexin', the way she wore them revealin' clothes and stumbled in at all hours."

"So how did she meet her husband?"

"Well, he was the grandson of a church elder. You see, they thought I would be a perfect match for him, so they invited my whole family over for dinner one day when he was visitin'. Praise the Lord, he didn't like me. I mean, he saw Sissy and he couldn't take his eyes off her."

"Did she fall for him right away?"

"Yes, Sissy was smitten. She stopped her partyin' and dressed all conservative. He was just about to finish seminary when we all met him, so Sissy knew if she wanted to be with him, she needed to clean up her act. Six months later, they were married, and he had his first church assignment, in Alabama."

"Was it always hard for her to be a preacher's wife?"

"At first she loved it. The church was a small one in a rural community, and they were just so grateful to have a pastor that they loved on her, and him, and made them feel real welcome. Then after they had been there a couple of years, she started to get restless and may have taken a second look at a bachelor in the area. They swear nothing ever happened, but the community got their undies in a bundle and Simon, her husband, got reassigned, this time as an associate pastor in a huge church in Texas."

"How did that go for your sister?"

"Simon was gone a lot, taking care of the flock. Sissy was still singin' in the choir, but she didn't want to lead any bible studies or nothin'. She started having babies and staying home with them more and more. Five babies later, she said she felt like a single mom livin' in the projects. Simon was gone all the time, the casseroles stopped coming from the congregation when the baby was three weeks old, and Sissy was about to lose her mind. Far as I know, now this is about twenty-five years later, she still wakes up in the mornin' and takes a nip from the bottle to jumpstart her day. She and Simon barely talk. He's got his own church now, still in Texas. She shows up on Sundays and smiles, wearing something nice, then she goes home and prunes her roses, cooks up dinner, which Simon may or may not be home to eat, and paints. That girl learned how to paint to keep herself from going stir crazy when the kids were all in school, except baby Brendon, he was still on the breast then. She is one of the finest artists I know. She's had a couple of shows down there in Dallas and works on some commission pieces for governors and such."

A couple cautiously poked their heads into the bay, and the nurses' conversation abruptly ended. "Mr. and Mrs. Valentine, is that right? Please, come in and be with your mother. I'll let the doctor know you are here."

Angela excused herself while the couple flanked the gurney and gently stroked the patient's pale skin.

<hr>

"IT SOUNDS like this Sissy had a lot of issues of her own and it's not just the being married to a preacher that is taking her down." Alecia took another helping of sweet, braised cabbage. "Girl, you really did this up right. You know I love my veggies, and this one is off the charts."

"I'm glad you like it. Bella taught me how to do it last

summer." Angela pushed the food around on her plate. "I think you're right. The whole time Teressa was telling me about her sister, I was thinking that this is so not my story. I even had to Google some to see if this was normal."

"What did you find?" Robert looked up over the top of his glasses.

"Of course, there are stories from disgruntled wives who feel like they don't have enough money or enough attention from their husbands. Then there are stories about women who love their role as partner to their husbands who followed their calling. It's a mixed bag. Besides, I can only give so much credence to stuff on the internet."

"How is it going with Trevor?"

"That initial glow hasn't worn off yet. I still get a thrill when I get a message from him. Our FaceTime is usually too short because I'm squeezing it in on a break or he gets a call or something."

"Have you talked to him about your questions?"

"No. I think it's too early. We are still kinda talking about the weather if you know what I mean. I really think that I have to find answers inside myself before I race to the altar with uncertainty."

"How are you going to do that? It's one thing to go to yoga or chant, but this, it's like you almost need a guide to ask those hard questions instead of leaving it to your own head." Robert pushed back from the table. "That was a fantastic meal, Ange."

"It's not over. I've got some dessert; I even made it myself."

Angela gathered up the serving dishes while Alecia and Robert stacked the plates and utensils. From the kitchen island, while preparing dessert and making coffee, Angela continued. "You know I went to an all-girls parochial school."

"Yeah. Was that just grade school?"

"No, all the way through high school. Anyway, I reached out to the alumni contact at the school and sort of explained what I was looking for. She emailed me information on a couple of women's retreats. I'm going to look into those. I think going away to intentionally explore my spiritual beliefs deeper, I'm going to get to some of the questions, if not the answers, that are bugging me now. I do think you're right, Robert, that I can't just be running the questions in my own head. I need to get them outside and explore them. It's not a matter of dating, or maybe eventually marrying a minister. My questions are really about who I am, what I want, and what I don't."

"That sounds like an excellent next step. Meanwhile, I really appreciate you cooking tonight. Everything has just been fantastic, and the company, as always, is delightful." Robert raised his coffee cup to the chef and his bride. "Next week our place again?"

"Oh, hey, that would be great, but I have another idea. Teressa and her husband sometimes perform at lounges around town, and they are singing on Saturday night. Care to join me?"

Robert looked to Alecia who enthusiastically nodded. "That's a yes for us."

"Fantastic. It should be fun."

16

———

he phone in Angela's scrub pocket buzzed, however, the four-year-old on the table needed her attention more. "So, Mom, I see that Devon is really upset. Can you tell me what happened?"

Angela made a balloon out of a glove to keep the young boy entertained while she evaluated him and got some history from the mom.

"He's a very active boy, as you can see. We were at the grocery store, and I asked him to get me a bunch of bananas. You know, like one bunch. When I looked back to see what was taking him so long, he was lying on the floor, dazed. He filled his arms to get a *whole bunch* of bananas, and while running back to the cart, he ran into a big ol' metal pole. I don't know how he missed seeing it, but I'm sure he was running as hard as he could."

"Hey Devon, buddy, I'm going to go get you some ice, okay? I need you to stay right here, in this bed, with mom beside you, and I will be right back."

While grabbing an ice pack from the nursing station, Angela paused a moment to check her phone. *Trevor. That's odd.*

She thought. *He never calls when I'm at work.* She made a mental note to listen to the message as soon as possible.

"You'll need to watch him for a concussion. Dr. Hayes reviewed all those signs with you, remember? Sleepiness, vomit…"

The mom held up her hand. "I'm familiar. Devon has two older brothers. We've been through the drill before."

"Okay. Call your pediatrician's office for a follow-up and we're here 24/7, if you feel you need to bring him back in." Angela extended a reassuring touch to Devon's mom. She couldn't imagine the amount of energy required to keep a household with three active boys together. It sounded overwhelming.

"Hey, Devon. How many bananas are in a bunch?"

Devon held up five fingers.

"Good job, buddy. You be good for Mommy, okay? And let her know if you need anything, alright?"

Angela waved to the pair as they walked, hand-in-hand, out of the ER.

"Chrissy, I'm going to take five. Are you okay to break down the room?"

"Sure, sure. Take ten if you want. You never break."

Angela stepped into the locker room, seeking a moment of privacy to listen to Trevor's phone message. "Hey Angela, it's Trevor. But you have caller ID and know that already. I have to go to Boston next week, and wondered, since I'll be close by, if I could stop and see you. No pressure at all, but if it's a possibility, I would really like to see you and want to consider that when I get my plane tickets later today. I'm happy to talk to you about it directly, but since you're working today, I realize that may not be possible."

She felt a heaviness in her gut. He sounded distant, not like the fun-loving, playful, Trevor she had gotten to know over the past few months. Angela punched in his number, but abandoned the notion before she hit dial. A text would do. She typed the words carefully. "Of course, you're welcome to stop by. I work Friday but am off this weekend. How do you feel about lounge singing? Planning to go with some friends to see some other friends sing on Saturday."

Realizing that she had never seen Trevor drink alcohol, choosing sparkling water or some other benign drink for his wine glass, she added, "Could cancel if that's not something you do. Either way is fine by me."

Trevor responded within seconds.

"I'll take the flight that lands at about 10:00 on Saturday morning. I'll look for a hotel nearby. Meet for breakfast?"

"Perfect. You can stay in my spare room if more convenient. I am happy to pick you up from the airport. Just send details." In a non-pastor dating situation, Angela wouldn't think twice about letting a date crash at her place if they were out late. She sighed. *Just one of the many ways I don't really know how to navigate this whole thing.*

"I accept your ride and we can talk about the other over breakfast. I look forward to seeing you."

Anxiety rose in Angela's gut. She washed her hands and smoothed her hair, pulled back into a high ponytail and braided. It was her usual work style and a reminder of where she was. *Suck it up,* she told herself. *Time to get back to work.*

***

"WHAT IS IT, GIRL?" Teressa asked as she and Angela walked to the lobby together at the end of their shift, before parting ways. It was their nightly ritual.

"What do you mean?" Angela thought she had masked the anxiety about Trevor coming and finished her shift strong.

"I mean, you always joking wit' me. You ain't been jokin', honey."

Angela waved off her friend's concerns with her hand. "I'm fine, really. Just looking forward to the weekend off."

"Well, if you say so. It's all good."

"Oh, hey, you're still singing Saturday night, right?"

"We sure are." Teressa stood tall and smiled, white teeth against dark skin. She wasn't a thin woman, but most of her weight was in her 40GGG, or so it seemed.

"That's good. I'm coming and bringing some friends. Do we need reservations?"

"You planning to eat there? If so, then yes, definitely. If you're just coming for drinks later, I can have a side table brought in for you up by the stage. They kinda move them tables around after feeding time, to make some room for them who like to dance."

"I'm pretty sure we will be eating there. If not, I'll send you a text."

"That's perfect." Teressa reached out and drew Angela in, patting her head as she did. "I know something's bugging you angel. You're going to be just fine. You always are."

"You're right, I will be. Thanks." Angela was reluctant to tell Teressa that the man who inspired the conversation about marriage to a preacher would be with her on Saturday evening. Somewhere on the internet, she had read that it's best not to disclose a dating relationship for sake of the pastor. She really didn't understand the why's. It probably didn't apply when he was 1500 miles from his congregation, but you never know.

"Okay, girl, you have a good night. We have just a couple more days here until we get a little time off. Go, get some rest so you can par-tay Saturday night."

Teressa strode out the front door and slid into the front seat of her husband's car; they kissed and drove off. Angela had watched that kiss hundreds of times over the years. She envied it and admired it, and them. They had faced a lot of adversity in their life together, but always faced the challenges together and supported one another. *I want that in my life,* she mused.

WEIGHED down by the intense day at work and Trevor's impending visit, Angela trudged wearily onto the elevator. As she pushed the button, a cheery voice called out. "Hold the elevator, please!"

She held the door open as Robert raced from the parking garage stairwell to the elevator and stepped in. ""Thanks, Angela. Woah! You look like you've had a rough one."

"Yeah? You don't. Why are you so bubbly?"

"Nice volley, but me first. What's up with you?"

"How much time have you got?"

"I'm so cheery because my wife is home early from work making one of my favorite dinners and she promised me a massage. I have from now until that massage starts. Just come home with me. You know Alecia won't mind."

"Are you sure?"

"You look like you could really use some friends. Yes, I'm sure."

"Okay, let me just rinse off and change my clothes. Give me twenty and I'll be up."

"Perfect. See you then."

"OH, Alecia, it smells heavenly in here."

"Happy to have you join us." Alecia passed Angela a stack of plates to set the table. "Robert says you're getting special company this weekend. Oh, hun. I know you're wanting time to sort things out for yourself. How are you feeling?" She had nursed Angela through perceived crises before and seemed to intuitively know what to say.

"Overwhelmed, uncertain, excited…a little bit crazy." Angela was really struggling to sort out her feelings. She really liked Trevor, but felt she had a long way to go to really know him, and even further to know herself. "I like him a lot, but I guess, the bottom line is I'm not sure I'm the right fit for his lifestyle."

"What, living on a ranch on the beautiful plains?" Robert chimed in. He loved his friend, and had seen her overthink and over feel too many situations. At least that's how his accountant brain saw it. "Let me say this, and I'll just say it only one time Angela. Sometimes you have to let go and let God. I don't think it's an accident he is coming to the city right now. Can you try to just lay down your shield and enjoy the weekend? You don't have to make any decisions about anything. Just have fun."

"You make it sound so easy. You know I'm a deep feeler. It's hard for me not to ruminate and second-guess."

"I know that. I also know that you have walked through the Program with me enough to know that change takes conscious effort and commitment. I think you want to be able to take it easier on yourself. Is that true?"

"You know it is," Angela easily admitted. "How many times have I told you that I spend way too much time and energy second-guessing myself? At work it doesn't interfere because I'm a damn good nurse and perform well under pressure, but when I'm home, after my shift, I relive and second guess my actions a lot."

"And has that served you well?" Robert was no coach or counselor; he'd just had enough counseling and been to enough AA meetings to have lived Angela's experience and witnessed many others with the same struggle.

"It might have."

"How so?"

"When I re-think things from work, I come up with better ways of doing things. More efficient, maybe."

"But did doing things the old way cause anyone harm?"

"No, of course not."

"So, all this worry about what could have gone wrong has not served you well, has it?"

"I guess not."

"Time's up," Alecia interrupted at just the right moment. "No more therapy. Dinner is served."

Robert went to his wife, put his arm around her and kissed her softly on the cheek. "Angela, have I ever told you how much I love my wife?"

"Only about a thousand times." Angela smiled. "And you should. She treats you like a king, especially when she makes you doro wat with the secret family spices."

"I'm glad you're here, Ange. You know I love cooking to share, like it's my gift to the world."

"Thank you, Alecia. Your cooking is definitely a gift that I am lucky to receive! Best Ethiopian food I've ever had."

<hr>

After a delicious meal with her wonderful friends, Angela felt full, comforted, and relaxed.

"Could you guys do me a huge favor? I promise I won't worry one more minute about it if you do. Could you please not mention to Trevor you know he's a pastor? I mean, I'm sure he'll tell you if you ask what he does, but I'd rather him not know I've made a thing of his vocation. It's kind of my personal issue, not his."

"Sure," they chimed in unison before Robert continued. "We have no need to bring it up. Let's just go and have fun. We've doubled with you before and had some good times."

Alecia chuckled. "Oh yeah. And some not-so-good times. Remember that Gary guy, the White supremacist? When he showed up and realized he would be dining with a mixed-race couple, he refused to sit with us and left!"

"That was the strangest ever. The friend who set me up didn't really know him. He was just a friend of a friend. I told her she needed to pick better friends. Just…weird." Angela wrinkled her face in disgust. "Trevor won't be anything like that, and if your experience is anything like mine, you'll like him, a lot."

17

"It's really great to see you, Angela." Trevor smiled sweetly as he gazed at Angela. "I like FaceTime and chatting, but there's nothing like the real deal."

He broke his gaze and silently gave thanks, before taking a sip of black coffee. This was entirely new territory for him. *Don't move too fast,* he warned himself. *She has to trust that you're not a player anymore.*

"I agree. I prefer seeing you in the fle…er…in person." Angela promised herself a stress-free weekend with Trevor. It had been a long three months since they had been together. The thrill in her gut was stronger than ever in his presence. She was perplexed though, curious about what brought him to the east coast. *Some caution is fine, but don't let your irrational fears scare him away.*

Trevor glanced around the busy restaurant with Scandinavian décor and linens on the table. "This is a cool place for breakfast. Is it one of your favorites?"

"If I'm having a leisurely breakfast or brunch with friends, yes. The Flying Swede gets rave reviews consistently. I found them after I read about them in the dining section of the newspaper years ago. Remember those things, newspapers?"

"Ha! Yeah, I think I do." Trevor took a long swallow of coffee then looked up at Angela. Without being too morose and rather matter-of-factly he began to explain, "You're probably wondering why I'm here now, and what's taken me so long to get here."

"I do wonder why you're passing through now, and no, I think we have talked enough since I got back here to know that life has been too busy for either of us to work in vacations."

"True, it has been busy. But believe me when I say, it's been hard not to hop on a plane and come see you." Being honest with himself, Trevor knew there was more to the hesitation to pursue her. He sensed that she needed time to let the thought of him in her life simmer.

"I just wish this was purely a pleasure trip. I got a call from my mom earlier this week. I know I haven't shared much about my father. Truth is, most of what I know about him I know from my mom. It's only been in the last couple of years that I've actually spoken to him, as an adult anyway. My parents, they never married."

Trevor took a bite of breakfast while gauging Angela's response. He hesitated before continuing, wondering if he would be able to finish eating after telling his story. "They met at a real low time in my mom's life. There were drugs involved and my dad eventually got in trouble with the law. He was in and out of jail my whole childhood. And when he was out, he was chasing a fix. He didn't see me or my mom, but through the grapevine she kinda knew where he was."

"Did you know his parents, your grandparents?"

"Apparently, he never knew his father, and my grandmother died before I was born. It's all kind of a tragic story. Anyway, my dad found Jesus in jail about eight years ago, just before he was released for the last time. By then, he was in his mid-sixties, and had several children by different women. He started working as a handyman while living in a halfway house. It's been over the past year that he got more and more ill. He had Hep C. This week, he passed."

Angela reached across the table and lightly touched Trevor's hand. "Oh, Trevor, I'm so sorry."

"Thank you. I think I knew the time was coming. I saw him early in the summer and was planning to see him just before Thanksgiving. I talked to him about a week ago. He wasn't able to hold the phone at that point, so a hospital aide stayed with him and held the phone while I talked. I had a sense it may be the last time we spoke."

"So, will there be a service for him?"

"There will be a celebration of life at the church he was going to before he died. It's near the halfway house where he lived and where he took on odd jobs. He once told me that these last few years were the most stable of his entire life. He had friends, had purpose in his work and volunteered as much as he could at the church, taking care of yardwork and repairs. He was genuinely happy and at peace. He had reconciled with most of his children. There are eight of us total. I'm somewhere in the middle. One of my half-brothers died as a result of addiction, and a couple others still struggle, but most of us have risen above and found purpose in our lives. I'm the only one that doesn't live within two hours of the service. All who can be there will be coming, along with the three moms that are still living."

Trevor paused, giving Angela time to process his crazy family. "I'm sorry if I overwhelmed you. I know it's a lot."

"If I were a local, down at the ladies' coffee table in Buffalo Ridge where families are fairly homogenous, it would be a lot. But living and working in the city, where families come in a lot of varieties, it's not alarming to me, except that it's your family. I mean, I did meet you in Buffalo Ridge, and the thought of this type of backdrop didn't dawn on me. That's not a judgment, just an observation." Angela took a breath, thinking carefully about how to prove that she wasn't put off by the details Trevor just shared. *Just be your kind and caring self. All else will dissipate and be a non-issue.* "How are you doing?"

"You know, I had a twinge of guilt about not being at his bedside. I mean, I would have been there for a congregant if they wanted. I do know that he had spiritual counsel with him and he believed that heaven was in his future, so I'm comforted by that."

The pair sat in mutual silence briefly, until the busy-ness of the restaurant consumed the silence. "Is there anything I can do, or that you need to take care of here in the city, before you head out to Boston?"

"No. I'm ready to relax and enjoy some time with you, even if it is brief. I think my old haunts, from spending time here before, are nothing I need to revisit at this stage in my life. A stroll in the park or whatever you want to do is just fine."

"Oh dear, Trevor. I'm sorry," Angela realized, given Trevor's new vocation, how inappropriate her evening plans might be. "I planned an evening out for dinner at a jazz club with friends. The entertainers there are friends. Given what you just shared, I'll rethink and…"

"Oh no! Please don't!" Trevor interrupted. "It's fine. I'm fine. A night out with you and your friends might be just what I need."

<hr>

THE AFTERNOON PASSED BY QUICKLY, with visits to Angela's favorite neighborhood haunts and quiet conversation. It was obvious that both enjoyed the other's company.

"So, what kind of place is this?" Trevor emerged from the spare bedroom and stood in Angela's living room sporting a black turtleneck sweater, black trousers and a tan blazer. "Is this suitable for tonight?"

"You look like you walked off the cover of GQ. You will be

the bell of the ball tonight looking so fine." Angela was feeling a bit bold and ready for an evening out.

"Well thank you, miss. I am no competition for you. Look at yourself with that lovely dress, and those heels. Yes ma'am, I do think you will be…"

The doorbell rang. "I can't wait to hear the rest of that sentence, but first, I'll let my friends in."

THE EASE of the afternoon continued into the evening. There seemed to be an immediate connection between Trevor, Robert and Alecia, which touched Angela deeply.

"Dinner was just fantastic, my friends, and the atmosphere here is sweet swank. I'm digging it." A smile lit up Trevor's face. "The velvet curtains and the leather booths over there, it's just cool."

"I also enjoyed my dinner, and a little bit of my husband's." Alecia kissed Robert on the cheek. "But now, I need to freshen up. Angela, care to join me?"

Alecia stood and held her hand out for her friend.

"Please excuse me." Angela joined her.

"I WOULD LOVE to be a fly on that wall, those girls chattering. Two of my favorite people in this crazy world. Honestly now Trevor, I can see why Angela likes you so much…" Robert didn't mince his words. He called things as he saw them.

"She said that?"

"Yes, but don't tell her I told you. Man, she's crazy about you. She's just, well, trying to figure herself out a bit. Give her time, man, she'll be good."

Trevor nodded seriously, but was unable to hide the happiness that Robert's words brought him.

MEANWHILE, IN THE LADIES' lounge Alecia freshened her lipstick between words. "Girlfriend, that is one fine gentleman, and I do mean gentle, and fine. If you let him go, you're a fool."

"You think so, huh?" Angela fluffed her curled hair and grinned widely at Alecia, who gave her a quick embrace.

"I do, and I think you do, too. Look in the mirror. You are all aglow, your aura is a mile wide."

Angela took one last look in the mirror and smiled back at her reflection before striding back to the table with Alecia. She was happy to see Trevor and Robert talking and laughing. Each stood and held out the women's chairs when they returned.

"Thank you all for inviting me to join you tonight. I'm looking forward to the entertainment. It's been a while since I've listened to live music that wasn't country."

Always curious, Robert asked, "Does that get old for you, living the country life without the culture and arts of the city?"

"You know, it really doesn't. I considered that when I moved back there. Surprisingly, besides the unique art in the landscape and skies of the plains, there are very talented artists of many media. There are world-class jewelers and carvers, painters, and musicians within miles of my home. But country music dominates the major gatherings."

This triggered a lively conversation, discussing the pros and cons of different versions of art.

"GOOD EVENING, ladies and gentlemen. Welcome to the Pink Flamingo. We are Teressa and Richie, also known as the Strolling Cats. More on how that name came to be later."

Teressa, in a flowing, peacock-blue gown with sequins

accentuating an already bold bust, glided across the small stage with mic in hand. Richie sat at the grand piano wearing a black tuxedo, with bow tie and cummerbund matching the sequined material of Teressa's gown. The first set began with a sultry jazz ballad that everyone recognized.

"The Fabulous Baker Boys!" Trevor and Robert pointed at each other across the table and laughed at their simultaneous outburst.

"Michelle Pfeiffer," Angela added while Alecia nodded in agreement.

The couples sat in admiration of the entertainers. Their performance was polished, with perfect timing. Generous applause followed the first song, which was immediately followed by another familiar tune, which Teressa embellished her own melodic tones and full range slides. Again, the audience responded with enthusiastic applause.

"This next song is dedicated to a dear friend sitting right there at that table…" Teressa pointed directly at Angela "…and of course, to the special friends joining her tonight. It's great to see you, angel."

Teressa crooned 'Our Love is Here to Stay' as Richie provided lively accompaniment. Guests rocked, dancing while seated, to the bouncy tune.

Trevor gently reached out to Angela's hand, resting on the table, and lightly squeezed it. Angela turned to him, and their eyes locked for a long moment. He released her hand and pulled his back. "She's fantastic!"

"She really is, and he is, too. Not only are they naturally gifted, but they have worked like crazy to develop a performance that people crave."

"They have succeeded."

When the duet took a break, they worked the room, greeting guests around the lounge. When they made it around to their table, Angela greeted Teressa and Richie with warm hugs and made introductions. The talented couple accepted the liberal compliments with grace.

Teressa, nestled up to Richie, addressed the table. "We just love that you are all here tonight and we got to meet you all, especially you!" She pointed at Trevor. "You be good to my girl. She's a special one."

Turning to Angela, she winked. "Love you, girl."

"Love you, too. Break a leg."

18

———————

"I can't thank you enough for letting me crash your date with your friends tonight." Trevor had taken off his blazer and sat comfortably on the sofa, legs crossed with one arm outstretched on the back of the couch. "I needed this. It felt wonderful to be with you and to share in this night."

Angela set a glass of water on the table in front of him and another in front of the chair nearby for her. "I'm so glad you could join us. I love them all. They have helped hold me together over the years."

"I'm sure you've been good for them, too. Robert said you were critical in his sobriety journey, and he is immensely grateful."

"I know you don't drink. Do you think that's for a lifetime? I mean, aren't you ever tempted to have a drink?"

"Sure. I liked drinking, but my genetics are stacked against me and it's not a fate I need to test. I had my fun, really, I enjoyed it a lot, but it was a social lubricant for me, and I've learned, and continue to learn, better ways of being me in social situations. I'm not offended or bothered by others drinking. It's no problem. Besides, it's one of the things a congregation looks at when evaluating my performance and if I just don't do it, there's nothing to talk about."

"That makes sense. How does your congregation feel about you being single?"

Trevor laughed. "How do you think they feel? I mean Buffalo Ridge is all about family."

"That's true. Do they have someone local picked out for you?"

Trevor laughed again. "If they do, they haven't told me."

Angela took a sip of water and pulled the throw pillow from behind her back so she could sit deeper in the chair. Pulling legs, now covered in sweatpants, up under her, she finally felt comfortable enough to ask that nagging question. "How does the dating thing work for someone in your profession?"

Trevor looked a bit surprised by the question. "It works like it does for anyone, I guess. I find someone I like who seems to like me back, and I spend time with them, getting to know them." He paused and playfully pointed a finger at her. "...you...getting to know you."

"So, we're dating?"

"Angela, we can call it whatever we want, but I'm clearly, at least it's clear to me, very attracted to you. I don't mean just the beauty of you...I mean the whole you. You're kind and generous and adventurous and loving. You have loads of integrity and a passion for your work. And I enjoy your company. A lot."

"You know I don't date recreationally, so that really begs the question I've had. Don't you need to have a wife that loves God like you do?"

"Now that's an interesting question. I'm glad you brought that up. When I was in seminary, I looked around me, at the married, sometimes twice or more married, students, the single ones and the dating ones and tried to figure out what the deal was with choosing a life partner. After talking to many of them and asking some really hard questions, I realized it's no different for seminarians and pastors than it is for others. There needs to be some common ground, strong communication, and willingness to constantly work on oneself, for both partners. None of the married students married because their spouse loved God the way they did. Some did meet through the church, but many did not."

"Isn't there an expectation that the wife takes an active role in the church?"

"That may come out as a congregational desire, but as for me, no. That's not my expectation. The church is my job, just like being a nurse is your job. Would the hospital expect me to come do work there just because you work there?"

"No, of course not, but I read that…"

He held up a hand. "Hold up. Where did you read this, and are there other rules of the road for pastors' girlfriends and wives?"

Angela smiled ruefully. "The only place I know to go for information like this. The internet."

Trevor laughed. "You're so cute. I'm really glad we're having this conversation. I forget that inquiring minds like yours like to have at least some answers before they ask the questions. I get like that, too. So, let's forget about what's on the internet. We get to write the playbook our way, okay?"

"Sure, but aren't there some basic guidelines?"

"I guess you could call them that, but I would not be here with you if you didn't already fulfill all those things. I mean, you're not going to be a bad influence on the youth of the church, you're not going to steal money from the church…"

"Of course not."

"Right, that's what I'm saying. If we do this dating thing and decide to take it further, like I hope you do, because I already know I'm headed there, the church would be lucky to have you as a member and I would be the happiest man around. I just don't see that you would not be supportive of what I do and my work with the church and outside the church. It is an important part of me; don't get me wrong, but I am more than just that job, as demanding as it is. And I think you need to know that. I'm essentially on call 24/7, but with a congregation the size of Buffalo Ridge, it's manageable and they are all very respectful of my time."

"That's good to hear. I would think…" Angela reflected on her conversation with Teressa. "That you could be gone a lot?"

"My pals who are assistant or associate pastors at larger congregations are the ones who really suffer. Those with families miss a lot of time with the kids. At Buffalo Ridge, I just don't have that struggle."

"You could have to move someday, couldn't you?"

"I suppose that's possible. If that came up, I, and my family, would have to make some decisions about our overall desires. Like, if your hospital has a sister hospital in Los Angeles, where you may not know anybody, you would have to decide if you wanted to continue to work for that company or fulfill your purpose to be a healer some other way."

"I think I understand. You also mentioned that you think communication and self-…how did you say it?"

"I think what I was referring to is the need to continuously reflect on oneself and work to be the best version you can be at any given moment in time. I am human and I have the failings of a human, but when I realize one of those failings, I have an obligation to address it. Maybe that means looking at the root within me that is causing me to do or be some way, or maybe it's a habit that I have that no longer serves me."

"I get it. Along those lines, I have been considering a couple of women's retreats – something to help me unravel some of the apprehension I've had about us. Honestly, just talking through these things with you tonight has helped me a bunch by putting the whole dating thing into perspective. I am still left with questions about my own religious and spiritual life. There is still a seed of it from my upbringing and schooling, but my worship time and rituals around faith are not there, and I don't feel called to reintegrate the same things back into my life."

"I hear you, and I'm glad you have a plan to investigate that further. I am, of course, available to listen and answer any questions you might have, from my perspective, but I feel you're doing the thing you need to do in a thoughtful way."

"On another note, unless you have more there…"

"No, I'm good, thanks." Angela shifted in her chair, stretching her legs.

Trevor looked over with concern. "Unless it's getting too late for you. It's after two already."

"I'm good for a bit longer. Your train leaves at five tomorrow, did you say?"

"Yes, and I have a ride from the train station in Boston so even if I'm a little sleepy, I'll be okay."

"Are you sure you don't want to find a church to go to in the morn…"

"I'm sure, but thanks."

"You had a question?"

"I did. Yvette mentioned that she invited you to Christmas with the Davies family. Do you know if you will be coming?"

"I had to work with the hospital to be certain there was enough coverage. I got the okay this week so I'll be looking at dates and tickets and stuff. I was going to talk to you about it but I really didn't want to get my hopes up and then not be able to go."

A look of contentment crossed Trevor's face. "Great! I'm happy to hear that you have the time off. It's about two months away now. I'm already looking forward to it."

"You'll probably be really busy during that time, huh?"

"There is a week there when it's really hectic, but we have lots of helpers at the church and they have a set group of activities that they want every year, so if I follow their script, all is well."

"Would I have a better chance of stealing some of your time if I come right before Christmas and stay until after New Year's?"

"Yes, but either way I will find time to be with you. It's very important to me. You, Angela, are important to me." Trevor leaned across the arm of the couch and took Angela's hand in his. "But now, I'm calling intermission. I think this would be a great time to take my leave and get some sleep. Please, sleep in tomorrow if you can. I can entertain myself if I wake before you do. Let's plan on eating out, my treat, when we are both up and moving about."

"Thank you, that sounds nice. Thanks again for our chat tonight. I feel more informed and on more solid ground now. I would love to be dating with you, Trevor."

Gently pulling her up from the chair, his arms enclosed her. He spoke softly into her hair. "Then dating it is."

The connection was so natural and mesmerizing that neither moved for several minutes, enjoying the pleasure and excitement of their connection. Finally, Trevor cleared his throat, kissed her gently on the forehead, and moved away.

Thoughtful as he carried the water glasses to the kitchen, he added. "Please, you don't need to keep it a secret. Bella and Yvette have done a good job of not really divulging anything, if they know anything. I assume you talk to Bella at least."

"I have been a little cautious about sharing too much. In fact, Bella doesn't know you're here."

He looked surprised. "Oh, please tell her... if you want. You two seem so close, I'm surprised that you haven't talked about any of this. It must be hard not to."

She shrugged her shoulders and nodded, thinking *I guess he knows me better than I thought.*

"Really," he spoke with assurance. "I'm prepared to manage rumor control if needed. I'm not scared of letting the congregation know we're dating. I mean, it won't be the topic of any sermon, but I also don't feel a need to hide it."

"That's a relief! I didn't really know how that would work if I came at Christmastime."

"I love that you are so thoughtful, but there are some things that just aren't worth the worry."

"Got it." She smiled wearily and moved toward her bedroom, reluctant to leave his drawing energy but too tired for more thoughts and emotion tonight. "Have a great sleep, Trevor. I'll see you in the…tomorrow."

19

---

*A*fter the brief visit with Trevor, Angela was inspired to jump into the personal growth work she had been talking about. She called the retreat centers that she was considering and was surprised to find how busy they were. Open retreat spots were months away, and the wait lists long. When the Whole Life Retreat Center in Maine messaged about an open spot in three weeks due to a cancellation, she considered it divine intervention and grabbed it.

ON DAY four of the retreat, Angela sat peacefully listening to Shira, the facilitator for the evening session. She was a lovely, petite, mature woman with eyes that exuded love. Angela had met her upon arrival at the Maine retreat center. One more day and she would return to home and work. "Okay, ladies. At this point in our retreat, we are moving into the Transformational Movement and Ceremony evening. Led by our shaman, we will learn to move the energy in our bodies, clear blockages and set intentions to let healing occur and bring the intentions into being."

The shaman took the stage. He guided everyone through breathing exercises and visualization, and then talked about vibration and energy moving in the body through the energy centers, the chakras.

"Now, as we move into the second, or sacral chakra, you may have feelings, or even visions, related to money, creativity, joy, sexuality, passion, or intimacy. We'll start with slow, gentle movements of the hips side-to-side. As you feel the energy move, the drummers will also feel the movement in the room and the tempo will change. Your movements may get wider or deeper. Here we go."

Five minutes into the pelvic circles, Angela was flooded with images of the last few minutes with Trevor. She had borrowed Robert's car and drove him to the train station. As they made their way from the parked car toward the platform, Trevor slid his arm around her, placed his hand on her waist, and stopped walking. Angela turned to him, and he pulled her in close. In full passion mode, he held her close while his mouth met hers and kissed deeply. Angela met his passion, giving in to the moment she had ached for.

As their lips separated and they regained some composure, Trevor gazed deeply into Angela's eyes and, still holding her close, said softly, "I loved our time together this weekend. Sharing more of my heart with you, and you with me shows me even more what I feel is so right. Angela…" Trevor wanted to be sure he had her full attention. "Angela, I love you."

Angela's heart and stomach fluttered simultaneously. She steadied herself against him. "I love you, too, Trevor."

Loud drumming intruded on the memory, bringing her back to the retreat center. She smiled to herself and let her hips swing. *Yep, the energy is flowing in the second chakra.*

"Angela, you look amazing!" Teressa gushed, happy to see her friend back at work looking relaxed and restored. "I take it the retreat was good for you?"

"Thank you. I do feel good. The retreat was fantastic. I'm still doing some soul searching, but between Trevor's visit and the time at Whole Life, I feel like I'm in a great place." Angela finished documenting a patient's condition in the computer and turned to head toward the next task. "Now, I'll work for a few weeks and then it will be time for me to go see Bella and Marco."

"And Trevor…" Teressa called to Angela as she walked away.

"And Trevor." Angela smiled back at her grinning friend.

Over the next few weeks, Angela found herself paying closer attention to the nursing assessment questions pertaining to religion and lifestyle. When she really listened to the patients, many of them elderly, she was surprised by how much importance the spiritual aspect of their lives held. They shared stories from their bat mitzvah's, baptisms, confirmations, visits from priests, and bingo in the church hall. Some younger people also expressed a connection with a church or group where they felt a spiritual connection. She lingered longer in the patient's room when the chaplains or personal priests visited, witnessing sacred space shared and the sense of relief and comfort experienced by the patients. As part of her own experience, she explored neighborhood churches, choosing a different one each week. While she didn't feel she had found the one for her, she felt welcomed in each of them. This exploration took her into Advent season. She found the anticipation of the season, felt through lessons, decorations and friendliness of the people, to be uplifting.

The third Sunday in December, just before leaving for

South Dakota, Angela found a church that felt especially good to her. During the service the congregation had a time to greet one another. "Good morning. I'm Beatrice. I don't think I've met you here before."

"Hello Beatrice, I'm Angela. This is my first visit to your church."

"Welcome. Welcome. It's nice to have you joining us today. Are you visiting or do you live in the area?"

"I live around here. I'm, well, I guess you could say I'm church shopping."

"I'd love to tell you more about us and what we have going on here after the service. I think you'll enjoy the service. Pastor Fred is the best!"

"Thank you. I'll catch up with…"

"If you would all return to your seats, we will continue with the responsive reading found in your bulletins and on the screens." Pastor Fred continued the service.

<hr>

SUNDAY EVENINGS HAD BECOME a time that Angela and Trevor set aside to chat, either before or after Angela's dinner with Robert and Alecia, which had also become a ritual.

"Here we are, the last Sunday evening before you hop on that plane." Trevor stated the obvious. Thoughts of her visit had consumed him more and more as her arrival neared.

"I know. It's wild how fast the time has gone, and I've been really busy. Like, even too busy to finish my Christmas shopping before I leave." Angela actually had only one gift left to choose, Trevor's, and that was proving to be the most difficult of all. "I bet your week coming up will be really busy, too."

"That's good, because I want it to fly by. Is Bella okay with me picking you up at the airport? I know you weren't planning to come until the 24th, but honestly, I'm glad the only ticket you could find was for the 22nd. Even that is a long time to wait to see you."

"You are sounding like a love-sick puppy whose people left him in the kennel." Angela laughed. "Honestly, it's so sweet. I'm looking forward to seeing you too… and the Davies clan. There is nothing like being face-to-face."

"Especially with your beautiful face. I have dreams of kissing you."

"Now you're just making me blush."

"You don't? I mean, you don't have dreams of me?"

"I don't think I said that. I do. Oh, Trevor, I do love you."

There was silence.

"Trevor, are you still there?"

"Oh, yes. I'm here! Just basking in the sunshine you sent in those words. Soaking it all in. Soaking you in. I love you, too, Angela."

The couple shared notes from their week past and anticipations for the upcoming week. They finished, as they had for the past several weeks, with a prayer. Angela's voice wobbled a bit. "Trev…I think I am ready to pray for us this time, if that's okay."

"Of course, my love, if you are moved, please, take it away." Angela could hear the smile in Trevor's voice.

"Dear God, Trevor and I come to you together in gratitude for the connection we feel. We ask your guidance as we explore our relationship, and humbly pray it will serve to know you more deeply. Please allow us to accept your nurturing and that of one another as we expand our hearts and courageously expose our vulnerable selves. Bring us strength to enjoy the journey, for all its joy and adversity, with your divine wisdom guiding us and radiant light shining upon us. Amen."

"Amen." Trevor broke the silence. "Angela, that was beautiful. I'm sitting here with goosebumps. Do you know how grateful I am that we met? Just think, if Bella had not moved to Buffalo Ridge we may have never met."

"That may be true, but honestly, I think if we were meant to meet, it would have happened somewhere in the world."

"Isn't that the truth. Well, I'm just so happy that it happened as it did and here we are. I will be at the airport on the 22nd at 1:45 with bells on."

"Thanks. I will have checked luggage so I probably won't be ready until after 2:00, if you just want to drive up and pick me up."

"Are you kidding? I'm not wasting one minute of this trip waiting for you in the car. I'll be there. Besides, I can help with the luggage."

"Oh, I can't wait! Until then, I'm pulling a couple of double shifts so don't worry about me if I can't text much."

"I will set all worries aside and focus on your arrival. I've got to do some chores yet tonight. Cows are calling me. Sweet dreams to you, Angela."

"And to you, Trevor. Love ya."

"Love ya. Good night."

20

___

"It's just like coming home, Yvette! You always greet me with wide open arms and a job to do." Angela giggled as she worked alongside Yvette. They were handing out mugs of cocoa to visitors at the annual Winter Wonderland Festival, complete with sleigh rides, hayrides, cookie decorating, a petting zoo and crafts for the kids. Bella and Steve had poinsettias, wreaths, and Christmas trees available through their greenhouse, and the dude ranch was booked with a large family spending their third Christmas holiday at the ranch.

"So, Angela, how was it to see your friend Trevor again yesterday?" Yvette slid up close to Angela and nearly whispered, as if she had a secret to share.

Angela never did tell Bella about Trevor's visit, for this very reason. She needed to see how she and Trevor, together, would introduce their relationship over the holidays. He brought her to Bella's after a warm greeting at the airport, complete with making out in the pickup in the parking lot. Angela felt like a schoolgirl. At the dude ranch, he walked Angela to the house and carried her things inside. He quietly closed the bedroom door to block the view of any bystanders and they shared a romantic hug and passionate kiss. That was yesterday. She would not see him again until this evening; he was taking her to his farm where he was preparing dinner. With stifled excitement, she calmly replied to Yvette's inquiry. "Of course, it was nice to see him. It was lucky he had business in the city and could pick me up. You all are so busy out here. How on earth do you get all this done and host the big Christmas dinner?"

"Honestly, we've got it down to a routine that works pretty well. It just takes a lot of freezer space for the cookies, and we feel really fortunate if we have some good snow, but we're okay even if there's no snow. We added Loretta, you know, our son Chance's mother-in-law, to the team this year. Since her husband Biggie passed away a couple years ago, we have brought her into the fold more and more. She is such a lovely woman and has really started to socialize and get back into life in recent months."

"That's great to hear. I remember meeting her on one of my early visits to Buffalo Ridge, and then I did see her working at one of the events last summer. Sweet lady."

"That would be her. She'll be joining us for Christmas dinner this year. My brother-in-law, Brian, will also be joining us. He has a ranch about 45 miles from here. Lost his wife a few years ago and this is the first Christmas we've been able to get him to come. Usually, he stays close to home with his kids, but this year they are going to the other grandparents' house in Iowa, so we got him to come."

"Here comes another big group." Yvette pointed to a caravan of vehicles pulling into the parking area. "Folks must like what we do here. We grow every year. In fact, by next year, we will probably need more help for the preparations. Can I sign you up?"

"I'll let you know, Yvette, if I am able to come earlier next year." Angela looked away, hoping that Yvette would not notice her blushing face. Her mind and imagination raced. *Oh the things that could happen in the next year!*

"You do that, sweetie." Yvette talked to some of the guests while Angela continued to hand out cocoa and direct the children to the cookie decorating tables on the Davies' large deck. The ranch looked like a scene Thomas Kinkade would paint, with an abundance of tasteful shimmering lights, wreaths adorned with red bows and balls, and greenery wrapped around the deck railing and poles.

During a lull in the activity, Yvette turned back to Angela. "On another note, I don't know if Bella told you, but we could really use help at the church tomorrow morning, if you're not too busy. We make up bags of candy and fruit for all the children and wrap a little gift for each of them. We give them to the kids after the children's program on Christmas Eve. Do you think you can help? I mean, I don't know what all you might have planned while you're here."

"Of course I can help, Yvette. I'll help Bella at the ranch first and then head over to the church after. I'm sure they have a vehicle available for me here. Can I contribute anything?"

"No, just your time. That's contribution enough."

***

"HELLO, BEAUTIFUL!" Trevor opened his front door before Angela could even knock. "Please, come into my humble abode."

He held a hand out to Angela and kissed her softly on the forehead as she crossed the threshold. "Let me take your jacket and hang it here."

Trevor gave a grand tour of his grandparents' home. "This river rock fireplace was built by my great-grandfather for my parents as a wedding present."

Angela studied the grand fireplace. "Wow! It is fantastic!

It's like a grand sculpture. And that mantle. What kind of wood is that?"

"That's cedar, and my great-grandfather carved the cabin and tree scene into it. He was an incredibly talented man."

Angela approached the mantle and studied the intense detail of the pine trees, log cabin, hills, and stream. "This belongs in a museum. It is exquisite."

"Yes, I'm very happy to be able to live with it here. It's quite special. I never met my great-grandfather, but he was loved by many. You may bump into some more of his work around the county. Even in the county courthouse." Trevor smiled as he watched Angela take in this favorite place in the house. "If you can imagine it, when this house was built it was a typical farmhouse."

Angela frowned. "Hmmm…I guess I don't really know what a typical farmhouse is."

"Let's just say it was a bunch of individual rooms, all with doors that could be closed when they didn't want to heat certain areas. When I inherited it, I set about remodeling it on breaks from school. I have buddies that work in construction, and they helped me." He pointed up to large, exposed beams in the ceiling. "We put those beams in. That way I could take down some of those walls that chopped the house up. Now, I can stand in the kitchen or sit in the dining area and watch the fire in the fireplace on a cold winter's evening."

"I love the open concept you have created here. And that all-white kitchen. Wow!"

"Actually, that was the last thing I remodeled, and I had input from Bella. I did that when I first moved back here."

"That looks like a Bella kitchen. Great job!"

"There used to be five bedrooms, but Bella talked me into turning a small one behind the kitchen into a butler's pantry. Would you like to see it?"

"Yes, I would love to."

Trevor opened a door to small room, perfectly lined with

pale moss-green glass-front upper cabinets, quartz countertops and dark grey base cabinets.

"As you can see, I haven't filled it up yet. I haven't really needed the extra glassware and roasting pans that I anticipate will eventually fill those cabinets, but I'm glad I listened to her. I can see how when I one day have a full house, we will need this space."

Angela blushed at the mention of 'we.' "Oh. It is so beautiful for a pantry."

"I'm glad you like it." Trevor ushered her out of the pantry and into another wing of the sprawling ranch house. "The house is built with the common areas in the center and then a wing on each side. In this wing there are two bedrooms and a bath."

Angela noticed the minimalist décor of the rooms. "Did your grandparents have a lot of stuff here when you inherited their home?"

"All the antique furniture here was theirs. I kept the beds and the functional things that I could use, but you may notice that I'm not big on a lot of stuff. I think it's because of my early years. Back then, everything I owned had to fit in a backpack because we never knew when we would have to leave a place, because it became dangerous, or we got evicted." Trevor paused. He hadn't thought about those early years for some time. H shrugged. "Or maybe I'm just a simple man."

"Maybe you have simple tastes, but I don't believe for a minute that you're a simple man." Angela walked up to Trevor and put her arms around his middle, pulling him close. "You are a very interesting man with a rich history and diverse tastes. I find you endearing and adorable." Trevor leaned in, touching foreheads then kissing the tip of her nose and trailing down to meet her lips for a deep, passionate kiss. He pulled away, caught his breath and with raised eyebrows said, "First… I want to show you the master bedroom in the other wing and then I need to get to the kitchen and check on our dinner."

Taking her hand, he guided her back to the kitchen and into the second wing. Through double doors they entered a large master suite. Across the room, Angela could see through a sliding glass door onto a deck and a view of the river breaks in the distance.

"I added on to this room when I was remodeling. It was a typical twelve by twelve bedroom with a tiny closet and no bathroom when I started." Trevor turned on lights as he entered a short hallway. "Back here you walk through a Jack and Jill closet and into the master bath."

"Trevor! This is absolutely stunning." Angela loved the all-white bathroom and the spacious closets, one empty and the other filled with Trevor's clothing.

"The only thing I wish I could have incorporated is a fireplace. I think, over by those two chairs, I could put in one of those electric wall fireplaces." Trevor pointed to two wing-backed chairs with peacocks embroidered in the fabric.

Angela walked over to study the stunning fabric.

"Those were the last pieces of furniture my grandmother bought. She was so proud of them. They used to be out by the fireplace, but I made this room big enough to have that corner over there to put them in."

"I can see why you would want to make a special place for them." Angela opened the sliding door and walked out onto the deck in the cold December air. "This would be another lovely place for an outdoor fireplace, if you wanted to cover part of this big deck."

"Look at you, Ms. Builder," Trevor chuckled, pleased to hear her ideas. He put an arm around her and guided her back inside to the warmth of the house.

"Ha! I've watched a few home-remodel shows on TV. Without that, I'd have no clue how to even start to envision a remodel. What you have done here, Trevor, is magazine worthy. It is absolutely stunning. It's almost retreat-like. How do you keep it so clean?"

"Well, I have to first confess that Bella didn't only help me with the kitchen design. This fall I had her come help me beautify the place, with you in mind. And after I visited you, I could see how spot on she was with her recommendations. And, as for keeping it clean, my mess is really outside with the animals, and I try to keep it there. There's a great mud room off the garage next to the house and I can generally leave the biggest mess out there. Otherwise, I don't make much of a mess in the house. I'm a pretty simple cook. Probably like many single people, I make a couple different dishes and they last me a week at a time."

"You probably have an entire congregation that helps keep you fed, too."

He padded his solid stomach. "That is somewhat true. I get a lot of cookies and things, but not so much the casseroles anymore. I got a lot of those when I first arrived."

"I thought that was just a stereotype, church lady casseroles."

"Nope, it's a real thing, around here anyway."

"Speaking of casseroles, I need to get to the kitchen and check on dinner. I hope you're hungry."

"I am, and it smells fantastic. What can I do to help?"

***

Angela was surprised to see Bella up when she got to their home. It was after midnight and baby Annie was having playtime instead of sleep time. She looked thoughtfully at her dear friend. "Tell me all about it, if you're okay with that."

"Bella, I am more and more crazy about this man with each passing day."

"I'm not surprised. I told you he's a great guy. What did you think of his home?"

"Of course, I expected an old, run-down farmhouse. I mean, only because it belonged to his grandparents and I guess

I just had this vision of something not updated. As you know, it is absolutely stunning. He did confess that he had your help.”

Bella chuckled. “Yes, he did. The kitchen is one of those dream kitchens you and I have talked about over the years. Not too big but wide open and easy to use.”

“That pantry, Bella! I don’t know how you talked him into that, but it is simply fantastic!”

“Is it still empty?”

“Completely.” They laughed like sisters who had a long-held secret.

“How was dinner? What did he serve?”

“He made chicken with mushroom sauce, rice, and a fresh salad. It was all perfect.”

“That was his great-aunt’s recipe. She was a caterer in the Denver area for a number of years and he fell in love with that. He’s made it for us too, and it truly was wonderful.”

“It was far more than I ever anticipated. Everything was.”

“Angela, you are absolutely in love with Trevor. I mean, it’s written all over you.”

“I am,” Angela honestly admitted. “But Bella, I don’t know if I can let this relationship go any further. I mean, the next step would be marriage, and I just don’t know that I can be a pastor’s wife.”

“If he were a doctor or a baker or a banker, could you be his wife then?”

“Given my hospital experience, I probably wouldn’t want to be a doctor’s wife,” she smiled ruefully. “But I wouldn’t have the same fears about being the wife of any of those men.”

“Then why is it different now?”

“I just don’t know if I’m Christian enough.”

Bella laughed, quietly, so as not to wake Annie who had finally fallen asleep. “Can I ask you something?”

“Of course.”

“Do you believe in Jesus?”

“Yes.”

"Do you believe he is your savior?"

"Uh, yes, I think so. At least I believe in the love that he taught."

"Then what's the question?"

"Wouldn't a good pastor's wife be equipped to lead bible study, sing in the choir, host a ladies' Psalm study and things like that?"

"If called to do so, it seems they could. But there is no written obligation in the Bible that you do any particular thing like that. You have a calling, Angela, and it would appear that is your work as a nurse."

"Right. And will I have to give that up? I know I love Trevor, and I love you guys. I just have to maintain a sense of who I am and not lose me. I don't know why I'm talking like this. It's not like he's asked me to marry him."

"I bet you've talked about it some, haven't you?"

"Yeah," Angela finally admitted to her friend. "Oh Bella, I've wanted to talk with you about it so many times! But knowing that he is your pastor and good family friend, I just couldn't burden you with all my issues."

"Oh Angela! How hard that must have been, 'cause I know how much I have depended on you in the past. I suspected something was up and I knew that it involved Trevor. But I know you well enough to realize that you would talk to me when you were ready."

"I'm more than ready," Angela smirked. "Yes, Trevor and I have talked about a variety of possibilities to continue our relationship, and it always seems to land on marriage. I used to think the hard part for me would be to move."

"What?! It would be hard for you to come play with Annie and Marco? And me? I don't think so."

"Of course that wouldn't be hard. The hard part would be leaving the work I love."

"You could still work. There are options. Like the clinic in town, and there is a hospital thirty minutes in one direction and an hour in the next. I know you've gone at least that far for some of your moonlighting jobs."

"Yeah, I guess so. Lots to think on. For now though, I'm going to stop worrying about it." Angela gazed lovingly at Bella and the sleeping baby. "You need to sleep like that wee baby and so do I. Tomorrow's another busy day. I'm headed to bed."

"Good night, love. Thank you for being my bestie, especially across the miles. My family and I love you dearly."

"Love you too, Bella. Night."

21

"Thank you for coming to help us today, Angela. It's nice to see you again."

Juniper, who Bella remembered from the spilled coffee incident months ago, was the organizer of the children's bags this year. She had one assembly line set up for filling the bags, and another for wrapping and tagging the gifts on tables in the church basement. "I think we could best use your help over here. We have these little notes with Bible verses on them that we put in the candy bags and then we tie them with a ribbon, so hopefully they don't start shelling the peanuts at least until they get outside the church."

"Great, thank you."

"You just slide right in here beside Becky. She's putting the candy in the bags."

"Hi Becky, I'm Angela."

"Yes, I've seen you here before. Nice to meet you, Angela. Did you bring Bella and that beautiful baby with you today?"

"No. Bella's got a full house at the ranch, so they stayed home to prepare dinner for the guests."

"They are always so busy, those people."

A woman across the table looked up and waved. "Hi there,

I'm Janae. Juniper's my mom. I'm here for the high holy days with my family."

"Hey Janae. I'm Angela. Where do you live?"

"We are over in northern California."

"Wow, that's quite a ways to come."

"Yep. Every year we make this trip to come see the folks and check on the ranch. So far, so good. They're about twelve miles up Dodge Creek Road, up there near where Pastor Trevor lives."

"I see."

"Say, I think I seen Bella's car up that way last night. She musta been delivering something to him. I know they got them poinsettias at the greenhouse."

Angela stayed silent about the car, and instead asked for scissors and ribbon, focusing on her project. *This is small town living*, she thought.

***

Angela stayed through the bag-making project, the hanging of banners in the church, and setting up for the following evening's children's performance. The church choir rehearsed in the balcony. The children would be rehearsing the following morning.

Finally, she excused herself. "Excuse me, please. I'm going to find the restroom."

"It's just down that hall there." A beautiful young mom, Julia, pointed in the direction of the first-floor education wing. "Bathroom's on the left, pastor's office on the right."

Angela hadn't seen Trevor all day, not that she was expecting to, but being in the same building she thought she might. As she was leaving the bathroom she paused in the doorway of his office.

"Hi there! Angela, is it? I'm Sheila, the pastor's secretary."

"It's nice to meet you, Sheila. Yes, I'm Angela. I was just wondering if Trev…uh, Pastor Trevor was in."

"Oh, I'm sorry you missed him. He went to Rapid City to see church members at the hospice house and the hospital. There was something he had to pick up downtown too, he said. I thought at first maybe it was his dry cleaning, but he was far too excited for it to be that. I think he'll be back in town too late to come back here, but I'm sure he'll be back tomorrow if you want to stop by. There's always last-minute prep to do during this season."

"Oh, I was just going to say 'hi'. It's okay. I'm sure I'll see him again before long." Angela thanked Sheila and backed out of the office.

Becky was putting her coat on before heading out into the South Dakota prairie wind and cold. "Angela, thank you so much for joining us today. It was great to have you and you're welcome to join us anytime. Let Bella know we missed her and I'm sure we'll see Marco in the morning at rehearsal for the children's pageant."

"Oh, what time is rehearsal in the morning? I'm sure Bella knows, but just in case I'm the one to bring him, I should probably know what time."

"They start rehearsal at nine, and the program starts with music from five-thirty to six followed by the children's performance."

"Great. One of us will make sure he's here. Thanks, Becky. I enjoyed the day with all of you."

WHEN ANGELA GOT BACK to the ranch, Bella was putting the finishing touches on dinner for the guests. "So, how did it go? Sometimes those ladies can be intense with all their questions and chatter."

"Good. Before I forget, Marco has rehearsal at nine tomorrow morning."

"Oh, man, I forgot. I was planning to serve these guests brunch tomorrow. Um…Maybe Yvette can take him."

"If you want, I'm happy to do it."

"Oh, of course!" Bella reflected on Angela's eagerness to drive on the ice and snow-covered roads. "Did you see Trevor today?"

"No. He was in Rapid City visiting members of the congregation at the hospital and picking something up, I guess."

"Hmmm…I bet it's something shiny," Bella mused teasingly.

"What do you mean? Is he getting a new truck?"

Bella chuckled, "Yes, I'm sure that's what he's picking up." She knew full well that he was at the jewelry store.

"He must've come into some money somehow, or has a great credit score to get a new truck and remodel that house the way he has. I've heard ministry doesn't pay that well."

"Yeah, I've heard others question his money situation, too." Bella was all too familiar with the town gossip, and tried hard to stay clear of it. "I never asked about where his money came from, and frankly, don't think it's my business. His ranch operation is too small to be bringing the kind of money he has had at his disposal and yes, I think his salary at the church is okay, but not huge."

"Neither here nor there to me," Angela announced firmly. "I've always paid my own way, as you know."

"Yes, Miss Independence, you have. And I'm darn proud of what you've accomplished."

"Why thank you, Miss Over the Moon in Love with Life on the Prairie. You are more happy than I have ever seen you, and I am happy for you."

The women put their joy and radiance to work feeding and

hosting the guests, spreading Christmas cheer with all their compliments and good tidings.

Easy conversation flowed again between the two as they cleaned up at the evening's end. "At first, I thought you were crazy for having guests over Christmas. But now I see how much and how joyfully you give, and how much they love spending their time together here, where they aren't worried about decorations and food and…"

"…laundry," Bella added with a groan before smiling broadly. "Plus, they give a generous tip every year and say they are so grateful not to have to do the cooking and cleaning and gladly trade cash for the time they get to dote on grandchildren and catch up with their adult children. So for me, it's giving and receiving. It's really a match made in heaven."

22

"Do you think I look okay? I mean, this dress isn't too low or too short?" Angela anxiously asked for Bella's honest opinion.

"I've never seen you care this deeply about revealing too much, Angela. What's up?"

"I've never been to church as Trevor's girlfriend before. I don't want to start off with the congregation thinking I'm some fly-by-night floozy."

"You? A floozy? Never! You look great, and proper." Bella passed Angela a stack of dishes to put on the buffet line for the ranch guests. They would be serving themselves while Angela and the Davies were away for the evening. "Besides, it's the children's Christmas pageant. The congregation will be paying attention to their children and grandchildren, not Trevor and not you. You might be better off to put jeans on like everyone else and then for sure they won't notice you."

"Seriously? Jeans?"

"Have you seen the weather out there? Yes, jeans. If the wind comes up while we're inside the church, we could be shoveling drifts just to get back home. It's up to you, but it's perfectly appropriate to put on some jeans."

"Okay. Thanks. I think I might have some pants that would work. Church has always meant a dress for me. Time to expand my thinking, again." Angela plugged in another chafing dish on the buffet table. "I don't know how you do it so perfectly every time, Bella. If I was putting this meal together, everything I made would be dried out by the time I served it. You - you made all the right picks."

"Years of experience working with caterers when I was going to culinary school and before that. I've developed a few tricks of my own, too."

"Well, this looks super. Tonight, we're going where, for chili and oyster stew?"

"Steve's brother, Jesse, and his wife Kerry's place. They have taken on that part of the family tradition. I offered, but thankfully, Steve said to spread the wealth. I'll help with Christmas dinner tomorrow."

"They are such a sweet couple. How's her vet practice going?"

"Amazingly well. She has two vets working with her now, one part-time and one full-time. They are very generous with the community, too. Very active, sponsoring kids' events. I imagine one day they will have a houseful of kiddos – enough to have their own softball team."

"LET US PRAY. Lord, we thank you for this time of fellowship and ask that we recognize, in your work through our children, the joy of the season. While we are all imperfect, we are Your love embodied. Share with us your patience as we explore the story of Jesus' birth through the eyes of your children. Amen."

The congregation pointed and giggled as the children walked, danced, twirled and stumbled up the center aisle, two by two, with wings, halos and wigs askew. One little angel stopped to tie her shoe and the shepherd behind her, who was waving to his parents, tripped over her. Sheep galloped like horses and one wise man dropped his treasure chest of chocolate gold coins, which rolled under feet and across the aisle.

An enthusiastic four-year-old shouted the welcome message from the front of the church. "I'm Cody. Welcome to our Christmas play. We invite you to enjoy the evening of angels, animals, Mary, Joseph, wise men and baby Jesus. My big brother Nathan will be the aerator…narrator." Cody's freckled-faced grin delighted the crowd. As he pointed out each group of actors, they waved to the audience, except for baby Jesus who was a plastic doll.

Nathan, a young teen, had memorized the entire script, including the bible verses. With the actors, who were often late to enter the scene, or talking to their neighbor, or waving at their family, his impatience was thinly veiled, until it came time for Bethany. Bethany had the important task of announcing that a babe was to be born and would be found wrapped in swaddling clothes and lying in a manager and he would be called Jesus. Bethany stood frozen amongst the group of angels, red-faced, with tears rolling down her cheeks. Nathan took her hand and brought her to the front of the stage. He held the microphone for her as she delivered her line in a shaky voice. When successfully completed, she released a powerful sigh into the microphone and wiped the tears on the sleeve of her Angel costume.

Marco was Joseph. He had no lines, but he got to walk with his favorite girl-friend, Marcella, who played Mary. He had to break up a disagreement during the performance when an angel snuck up to the wooden manger filled with a local farmer's straw and stole the baby Jesus. Marcella grabbed the doll to rescue the pageant and Marco stepped in. He reached down and picked up a stuffed animal, a prop near the manger, and gave it to the wayward angel.

Angela joined the rest of the congregation giggling about

the antics on stage. She leaned over and whispered to Bella. "He's a peacekeeper already. You gotta be proud of that boy. I sure am!"

<hr>

"That was an amazing performance, Marco."

"You did a great job, honey."

Marco joined the family in the entryway after the performance. He collected his candy bag and gift, and then enthusiastically encouraged everyone to leave.

"Uncle Jesse, I'm starving. Will dinner be ready when we get to your house?"

"Yep, Marco, it is ready. Auntie Kerry made sure it was all ready before we came to watch your play. You did a good job there. Did you have fun?"

"It was okay. I asked to be Joseph because he didn't have any speaking lines, but I still had to sing."

"You don't like to sing, Marco?" Pauline attended the performance without Chance, who was at the airport picking up Stella, the Davies sister.

"Oh, it's okay, but the girls are kinda shrieky."

The adults laughed as they bundled up and left the church.

"See you all at Jesse and Kerry's." Yvette called out to the group as they dispersed to their own vehicles.

<hr>

"Auntie Angela, have you tried the oyster stew? I like it this year. My tastebuds must be maturing."

Stifling a laugh, Angela responded, "I'm sure they are, just like the rest of you. You're getting so tall, and you've always been so handsome. Come give your auntie a hug."

Angela looked around at the Davies couples. *Living displays of God's love in action*, she thought. She was sad that Trevor couldn't join her, but he had other obligations tonight and would be joining them tomorrow.

"Hey, Angela, have you met my uncle Brandon? Well, he's not my uncle yet, but I'm sure he will be someday. He and Stella live in Arizona."

"It's a pleasure to meet you, Brandon. I'm Angela. I've heard great things about you, and of course I've met your beautiful fiancé, Stella. What a force, eh?"

"She is a force, indeed, just like all the Davies kids. They've all paved great paths. You're Marco and Bella's friend from New York, right? I know Stella had a good time with you at another family event you were at. We don't get out this way often. Stella prefers the isolated spaces where we live, but she loves her family. It's quite a dance."

"That's right. This little guy used to be a city dweller. Spent his early years in my apartment."

"Well, Bella sure seems happy out here, and I know Steve is. I understand that he was so devastated when his first wife passed away. The whole family worried about him. He's so proud of his family." Brandon ruffled Marco's hair. "This guy is proving to be quite the cowboy I hear."

"I am. Uncle Chance even said so, and he's a REAL cowboy!"

"He sure is buddy. Has he shown you his buckle collection? I bet it's huge."

"Takes up one whole wall in the tack room. He's got some cool bull riding pictures, too."

"I'm really happy he's there to help you out, bud."

"Yeah, me, too."

"Nice meeting you, Angela. I'm going to go get some of that oyster stew that Marco is bragging about."

"Have one for me, too." Angela raised her half-eaten bowl. "I prefer the chili."

Angela found Yvette sitting quietly in a corner, observing the room packed with precious family, and sat down beside her.

"Are you ready for tomorrow, Angela?"

"I guess I'm ready. Presents are wrapped and ready to bring to your house. And how about you, Yvette? Do I need to bring anything else?"

"Oh, no. Just your wonderful self." Yvette had an extra sparkle in her eye tonight.

"It must be great to have all four of your children and their partners home together."

"Oh, it sure is. That's the most wonderful Christmas present I could have. It's been a while. And you! I consider you one of my kids now too, just like Bella and Kerry, Pauline and Brandon."

Angela was so touched that she became teary. She reached in and embraced Yvette in a one-armed shoulder hug. "I love you, Vette."

"I love you too, honey. Thanks for giving this family a chance."

"You're such good folks, how could I not? You make me feel a part of something, unlike anything I ever experienced before, except with Bella and Marco. More than even with my own family."

"Oh, sweetie, you're going to make me cry. I'm looking forward to seeing Trevor tomorrow. How about you?"

"Yvette, are you getting at something?"

"The whole town knows you're an item."

"What?!" Angela cried out. "I haven't told anyone – not at coffee or the church. How?"

"I think he let it slip to a buddy and it kinda spread like wildfire."

Angela laughed anxiously. "Really?"

"Oh, yeah. And he didn't seem to feel badly at all when people started asking him about it. In fact, he seemed right at home with the idea. Sounds like you had a really nice dinner there the other night, too."

Angela drew in a breath. "Now I know I didn't tell you about that and Bella swore she wouldn't say a thing."

Yvette laughed. "Small town, remember? Someone saw Bella's car in the driveway and put two and two together." She reached out to hold Angela's wrist. "I am so happy about all of this! It's okay, you can laugh. This is the way it is. Can't have any secrets around here."

"No, I guess not. Church should be interesting tomorrow."

"I think the focus will be on Jesus' birth. No need for you to fret about anything else…" Yvette paused, suspensefully, "until Christmas dinner, anyway."

"Oh, boy."

"It's all good, hun. Don't you worry one bit. We like our people to just be real. Just be yourself and everything will fall into place."

23

" . . . *A*nd as I end today's sermon, I want to emphasize just a couple of lessons that come from the Christmas story." Trevor's voice from the pulpit was confident and caring. "As we have learned in the sermon series over recent weeks, Joseph was a quiet man when it came to speaking words, but with his behavior he spoke loudly of pure love through his willingness to live selflessly and take up the task of serving and loving others, as he did Mary. In this season of love and joy, I invite you to find everyday ways you can transform your own life by bringing that joy forward. In the scripture reading today of First John 1:1-4, we read about incarnation, and we sang about it in *Hark! The Herald Angels Sing*. Looking at incarnation as transformation, we can carry the mystical lessons of Jesus' birth and the surrounding story, and actively live the entire holiday with a sense of joy as we exchange gifts, greet our loved ones and neighbors, examine our sorrows and opportunities, and embrace the true meaning of the holiday as we wish others a genuine **MERRY** Christmas."

The service concluded with *Silent Night* by candlelight, as neighbors spread the light of Christ through sharing the flame from one candle to the next throughout the church. Joyful greetings spread throughout the congregation as they met across the aisles, in neighboring pews, in the choir loft, the entrance and spilling out onto the sidewalk.

Children excitedly shared about gifts they had received the evening before, if they opened any, and what had been left for them under the tree overnight.

"Santa brought me a BB gun," one boy shouted with excitement as he threw himself into the snow on the lawn to make an angel.

"How about you, Marco, did Santa bring you a present?" a friend of Yvette asked as she pulled his stocking cap over his left ear.

"I got a really cool remote-control truck. I got to take it out on the deck. It can climb!"

"That sounds awesome. I hope you have a lot of fun playing with it. Are you going to have a big Christmas dinner today?"

"Huge. I mean, did you see our family in church? We took up two pews! And grandma Vette and grandpa Dan have a huge pile of presents under the tree. Some are even for me!"

"I bet you have a lot of fun with everyone today. Be sure to help grandma whenever she needs it, okay? I know she sure likes it when you help."

Yvette stepped in on cue and put her hand on Marco's shoulder. "This grandma couldn't ask for a better helper. We better start making our way back to the ranch, Marco. I saved a job for you to do today for dinner, and another one involving presents."

Marco looked up at her, eyes dancing with excitement. "Let me guess, pour water in the glasses and water the tree."

"We aren't going to water the tree today. There are too many presents to get to the watering stand. I was thinking that later, when it's time to open gifts, you can help me pass them out. You can read cursive, can't you? I think some of the tags are written in cursive."

"I can, mostly. If I need help, I'll ask you or mom or auntie Ange to help me. I can do it."

Yvette gave her friend a Christmas hug and ushered Marco out the door, where they met up with the rest of the family.

"Okay, let me get a picture of this whole family right here in front of that stained glass window. Go find everyone Marco."

ANGELA REMAINED QUIETLY in the pew as the church emptied. She was in awe of Pastor Trevor, the man who led this congregation. Her heart ached with love for him. Her body yearned for more contact with him. Yet her mind still whirled with doubt and fear. How was it possible for such a handsome, caring, compassionate man to love her? Was it possible for her to exist within this tight, sometimes overbearing, community without losing herself, her true being?

Lost in thought, she barely noticed when a man sat next to her until he spoke. "Hey Nurse Angela."

Years of nursing had her trained. She turned her attention to him quickly with a curt, "Yes?"

He looked familiar, but it took a moment for recognition to set in. "Oh my gosh! You're the EMT – Evan."

He smiled, delighted that she remembered him. "I have wondered about you since that crazy accident day. As a matter of fact, I started to believe that you were a figment of my imagination – an angel who just showed up that day to save those people and then disappeared. I am thrilled to see you here today."

"What are you doing here? I mean, here in this church in Buffalo Ridge?" Angela asked.

"Moved to a small place just outside of Buffalo Ridge a few months ago with the family. We thought it might bring some good country living, and hey – I can commute easily anywhere in this area. I'm not a usual church-man, but my son wanted to see his friends in the pageant yesterday, and of course we had to return today. I thought that Pastor Trevor was familiar, but couldn't quite place him until I saw you. And you? From around here?"

"Actually, I'm an ER nurse from New York." Angela saw Evan's raised eyebrows so hurried on to explain. "My best friend is Bella Davies from the Davies Dude Ranch. Have you heard of it? Great place."

"I have," Evan acknowledged. "I think I've once helped a Davies brother to the hospital after a rodeo?"

Angela smiled. "Probably Chance. Well anyway, Bella is my best friend. I come out here to visit and help her, and the Davies family has kind of adopted me."

It was Evan's turn to smile. "And I'm thinking that Pastor Trevor has as well."

"Yes, I think he has," she freely admitted.

"Well Angela, I hope that is a good thing and it brings you here soon. From my short experience with you, you are a damn good nurse. Oops- sorry Lord for such language – forgot I am in church. There have been a few times on the job in the last few months when I wished you were around to advise me. This area sure could use your expertise and your patience."

"Seriously?" Angela asked sincerely. Evan sensed her turmoil.

"Seriously," he replied. "I believe there will always be a place for you."

And with that, the whirling in Angela's mind eased. Evan continued, "Look me up when you're back here. I'll leave my info with Pastor Trevor. Oh, and by the way, found some very nice boots at that accident site and took them home. I assume they're yours? Not quite my style and don't fit my wife, so I'll leave them here too. Now I really must find my family, who are probably freezing outside in …"

The sound of running feet and Marco's excited voice broke

in. "Auntie Ange! I've been looking for you everywhere! We need you for the family picture. Come on!"

Evan laughed as they both stood. "Duty calls for both of us. See you around Nurse Angel."

"Ha! That's funny," laughed Marco as he grabbed her hand and pulled her down the aisle. "Nurse Auntie Angel. Let's go!"

Angie paused and turned back toward Evan. "Ever hear the outcome of that accident?"

Evan smiled. "A true miracle, I guess. Everyone survived, including the baby."

"Oh good! Merry Christmas Evan." Angela beamed. "OK Marco. Race you, but we have to fast-walk.

<hr>

OUTSIDE, Trevor was holding Dan's phone, aiming the camera and trying to herd the large group into one bunch of three rows, as the last of the straggling parishioners wished him a Merry Christmas. Marco pulled Angela in close beside Bella, and Steve with Annie in his arms.

"Ok, on the count of three, say 'pizza'," Trevor called out. "One, two, pizza!"

Trevor handed the phone back to Dan and turned to shake hands with a couple that was waiting for him with a gift in hand.

"We won't keep you long but wanted to be sure we got this directly into your hands. I know you cook, but you said you weren't as confident with your desserts, so we made you one. If you can't use it up today, it can certainly go in the freezer for another time."

Trevor thanked the couple and shook their hands heartily as he took the gift from them.

"It's a white chocolate raspberry cheesecake. We hope you

enjoy it," the wife said, taking her husband's arm to steady herself on the snowy walkway.

Angela held back to talk to Trevor for a minute before joining Steve, Bella and the kids in the car.

"Hey, you." Trevor put his arm around Angela and walked with her back toward the church doors. "Gosh I've missed you, and you've been so close by! I've been looking forward to seeing you. How are you?"

"Good, good. Bella's waiting for me, I just wanted to say hi."

"Okay. Well, if you want to ride out with me, you can. I just need to close up the church and change my clothes for dinner."

"Sure, let me just tell them."

"Awesome. I'll be in the office, just come on in when you're ready."

———

Angela returned shortly to find Trevor taking care of church business with a few regulars who hung back to help clean up.

"Pastor, that was a fantastic Christmas message."

"Sure was. It's refreshing to get the Christmas message reframed to today's world. You really have a knack for that. I'm going to go out and spread Christmas cheer. I hope you have plans yourself, Pastor."

"I sure do!" Trevor answered happily. He reached out and shook their hands. "Dave, Paul. Thank you for your unfailing support of me and this church. For as long as I can remember, from my childhood days here, and far before that I'm sure, you have been pillars here, always giving of your time and gifts. I appreciate you both so much."

He looked over to the doorway as Angela moved into the office. "Gentlemen, I believe you both probably know Angela."

"Oh yes. Hello Angela. It's so nice to see you again, and at Christmas to boot. The Davies family is excited for you to be joining them." Paul stepped forward and took Angela's hand in his.

"As am I, Paul." Trevor's face was beaming. "Angela is my special friend."

Paul turned back around to Trevor. "Well, is that right?!" He put his hand on Trevor's shoulder. "Congratulations, Trevor. I am happy for you and wish you both the merriest of Christmases."

"Me, too. I'm Dave, Angela. It's a pleasure to meet you. I think I've heard of you, but I move a million miles a minute and not all the information sticks, you know."

"I understand, Dave. I'm a nurse in a very busy ER in the city and if I tried to remember everything, I could never function long-term. It's a real pleasure to meet you and I do hope you have a Merry Christmas."

"Thank you. Gotta run, got three invitations for Christmas meals today. That's when it's fun to be a bachelor when others are doing the cooking." Dave disappeared out the door, throwing his hat and trench coat on before anyone could say another word to him.

"I've got to get home, too," Paul spoke as he made his way toward the door. "We have family coming in this afternoon from the city and parts east, so I'm going to go help get things ready, although I'm sure it's mostly taken care of already. We'll see you next week sometime, Trevor. Welcome back, Angela. Have a merry Christmas you two."

"Those two men are fantastic, and the best of friends to each other," Trevor spoke as he tidied his desk and filed the last of the papers there. "They have taken me under their wing and provide great constructive feedback. I'm not sure every young pastor gets that level of support, and I am so grateful to have it."

"That's fantastic. Sounds like they have been here a long

time and really know the lay of the land. That's got to help a great deal."

Trevor pulled a down jacket on over his jeans and dress shirt. "It's been a fantastic bonus for me. Shall we?"

He held his arm out for Angela, who gladly snuggled up next to him and slid her arm under his. She felt somehow reassured and excited by Trevor's openness to share their relationship with trusted mentors.

***

"CAN I kiss you one more time before we go in? I am just so happy to be spending the day with you and your surrogate family here."

Trevor, loaded down with bags of gifts, somehow wrapped his arms around Angela and pulled her in close. His mouth almost met hers when the door swung open.

"Welcome! Welcome!" Yvette called out. "Welcome to the great Davies Christmas Dinner. Come in, come in. It's cold out there."

"Uh, sure, thanks."

"Hey, Yvette."

Trevor and Angela stepped in and wiped their feet on the extra-large rug in place for all the guests. Yvette was in her glory – giddy, excited, and in charge.

"Let me just lay out what happens here. First, come in and deposit your coats in there on the daybed in the office." Yvette pointed to the open door at the end of the hallway on their left. "I see you have presents. You can deposit them under the tree. When you're ready for an appetizer, come on out to the bar in the kitchen and fill your plate. Of course, we have a load of appetizers, so fill your plates many times. At about two, we will gather around the tree. It's a tradition here that everyone reads a poem or a story or shares a Christmas memory with the group. If you need inspiration, there are some books piled up on top of the piano. Steve will lead us in some carols. We will have dinner after that and after dinner, while we have coffee and dessert, Marco will distribute gifts and we will open them."

"Wow, that's quite a production, but I should expect nothing less from you, Yvette." Trevor held out the cheesecake he received at church. "Here's another dessert. The Masons gifted it to me today."

"Fantastic! Midge makes the best scratch cheesecakes. Thank you so much for sharing with us. I'll be sure to send leftovers home with you, if there are any."

"Oh, please don't." Trevor patted his belly and snickered. "I have a freezer full of goodies from this season already."

———

ANGELA AND TREVOR made the rounds, greeting everyone as they roamed through the house. Marco was the only child, but his uncles kept him entertained, or he them, as they played games and tried out his new remote truck.

Angela marveled at the variety of food laid out on the kitchen bar. "Yvette, this appetizer station is a feast in itself."

"Well, you and Bella, I know, made several of the things - the phyllo triangles, the caviar mold, and those incredible elk meatballs. I have to get that recipe."

"That's the first time I ever made anything like that, to be honest. Wild game is pretty foreign to me."

"That sounds like something I need to taste." Trevor looked over the variety of selections. Angela pointed to the crockpot with the meatballs. "They are pretty tasty, if I must say so myself. I hope the guests at the ranch are doing ok."

"I know you ladies put brunch stuff out for them. Bella stopped by there a little bit ago and put the appetizers out. She plans to go back later. They were planning a later dinner, so it will work out perfectly. They were going snowshoeing this afternoon and the big screen is set up so they can watch an oldie Christmas movie. That's kind of one of their traditions." Yvette was scurrying around the kitchen, stirring pots on the stove and checking on the turkey in the oven.

"This place smells so good, Yvette," Trevor remarked between bites. "It reminds me of grandma's kitchen when I lived out on the ranch with them."

"Your grandma was one of the best cooks I ever knew. She made everything, and I mean everything, from scratch."

"Is that right?" Angela didn't know much about his grandparents.

"Even hamburger buns and pickles. Seriously, everything. One amazing and hard-working woman. Used to love sitting around and listening to her stories. She and your grandpa sure saw a lot in their early days here. I hope you had the chance to hear some of those stories too, Trevor."

"I did and wrote some of them down. I had Gramma record some of them on old audio tapes, too. Real treasures."

Trevor took his full plate out to the living room, joining many of the other guests. Angela went to find Bella.

"Hey, Bella, where is sleeping beauty?"

"She's making her rounds with the aunts and uncles out there. She's been such a good girl today. I think she's going to be pretty tired by the time the day is over, though."

"Maybe you'll get a full night's sleep then."

"Fingers crossed. It's so nice to have Trevor here." Bella and Angela stepped into a corner, away from the commotion in the kitchen and living rooms. "He is so crazy about you; you know that, right, Angela?"

"Yes, I do. I think I can count on one hand the number of days we haven't spoken in the past three months, and he never hangs up without telling me something he loves about me. It's just the most precious thing."

"He just beams having you here, in his community."

"He told a couple of the elders that we were a couple

today, when we were in the office after the service."

Bella laughed. "They have to be the last people to know, Ange."

"Well, they acted surprised, but maybe they weren't. They did seem really happy for him, though."

* * *

THE PRE-DINNER TIME of sharing stories and poems was intriguing. Angela was surprised at the honesty and heart of each story, even that of the men. She was all ears, as was everyone in the room, when Trevor spoke of his eighth Christmas.

"I share this story, not for sympathy, but for us to remember in our hearts, those who are far less fortunate during the holidays. That year, there was no Christmas tree. My mother didn't have money, and she had been in and out of the hospital with infections from being so malnourished and drinking and drugging. I'm not talking out of school here. If she were here, she would tell you the same story, but with tears in her eyes, because she has so many regrets. When Christmas morning rolled around, I woke up to a mother who had stayed up all night, complete with dark circles under her eyes and still dressed from the night before. With watercolor paint, she had painted a Christmas tree on the wall, watercolor so she didn't get in trouble with the landlord. She had borrowed cocoa, peanut butter, and oatmeal, each from a different neighbor, to make my favorite cookies. Under that watercolor tree were eight gifts, all wrapped in paper towels from the 7-11 bathroom and taped with Mr. Yuck stickers from the educational poison control goodie bag we got from our last public health visit. Seriously, it's okay to laugh. I do." Trevor paused and smiled, a confident smile far beyond tragic past circumstances. "My mom struggled, as you all know, but I never doubted that she loved me. I still remember exactly what was in those eight packages. Two of them were those hospital grippy socks. She was a frequent flyer at the hospital, and managed to keep two pair that were never opened. I did wear them. In fact, they came in handy on cold winter days in holey boots. Another gift was an origami dragon. One of the hospital aides had taught her how to make it. I still have it. It's in my office. There was a half-used bottle of cologne, probably the most absurd of the gifts for an eight-year-old. One of her many boyfriends had left it behind and rather than throw it out, she saved it for me. There was a handwritten coupon for a lifetime of daily hugs. That coupon actually expired by that New Year's Eve, when she disappeared and I didn't see her for three days."

Yvette wiped away a tear, while several others sucked in their breath.

"Where did she go, was she in the hospital again?" Marco was listening intently to a child's life so different from his own.

"To this day, I don't know, Marco. There are some parts of my mom's life that she would not share with me as a child, and as an adult, I don't need to know."

"I'm sorry Trevor that you didn't get to have your mom every day."

"Thank you, Marco, but as different as my life was from yours, my mom still showed me she loved me. It was just in ways different from your mom and dad. Okay, let's see, I think I told you about five of the gifts. The other three were a tiny bible that a chaplain at the hospital gave her, a Christmas tree ornament she made out of paste and flour and decorated, and a gift the Salvation Army provided. It was like a Furby. You remember, one of those robotic animal type toys that would respond to your voice? It was really hip at the time, and I was on top of the world to open such a lavish toy. And that's it." Trevor was done and ready to move on.

"Thanks Trevor. Your story helps keep things in perspective. I think the important thing is your mother loved you, regardless of how much money she had to spend on you."

Yvette wanted to move things along so the turkey didn't dry out, without disregarding Trevor's moving story.

"That is absolutely correct."

"Angela, I think we are now to you, and you are the only thing keeping us from dinner."

"No pressure, huh Yvette? My story is really short and sweet. I remember your third Christmas, Marco. You and your momma were at my apartment, and that year all you wanted for Christmas was a hover board, and if you couldn't have that, you wanted a baby brother or sister. You were clearly too young to have a hover board and a baby brother or sister was not in the cards, so your mother got you a…"

"Oh yes! I admit it!" Bella interrupted. "Hover boards scare me to death, even now! I got him a Candyland game to play indoors and a little plastic scooter, with a helmet of course, that we could take to the park. Seemed a lot safer."

"And he had to wait a while for me to be around for that baby sister," Steve chimed in as he lovingly hugged Bella.

"Yeah Mom. It's okay. I'm sure I liked them both. And Dad and baby Annie are worth the wait." The family laughed and patted Marco on the back for being such a good sport.

"On that note," Yvette announced, "I'd like to invite you all to the table. Dan, you know where everyone goes. Can you please help them get to the right seat while I pull out the wine?"

"Oh, none for me, please," Kerry and Pauline said in unison.

Kerry looked at Pauline, who looked back at her, both with twinkles in their eyes and mouths agape.

"Um, ladies, the only reason someone doesn't have wine in this house is if they are…" Stella started stating the house rules when Yvette and Loretta jumped in.

"Pregnant!" Yvette rushed to Kerry while Loretta rushed to her daughter, Pauline.

"Where's my video camera when I need it?" Chance

shouted.

"No worries, bro, I got you covered." Steve still had his camera recording from the storytelling.

"Are you two honestly expecting?" Bella asked, feigning incredulity that she had missed the telltale signs. "How did I not know? When?"

Kerry and Jesse responded "April" while Pauline and Chance simultaneously said "May."

The room roared with congratulations and celebration.

"Okay, okay, we've got to get to this turkey before it's jerky. Please take your seats." Yvette was excited, but also concerned about her Christmas dinner. "We don't want to ruin this extra-special dinner with rotten food."

Talking excitedly, the family took their assigned seats. When they were all seated, Yvette asked Trevor to bless the food, which he gladly did.

As they were clearing the dinner plates before gifts and dessert, Trevor pulled Bella aside.

"You know my plans for today. Would it be terribly tacky if I still followed through? I mean, can there ever be too much excitement and good news?"

"You're still good, Trevor. In this family, the more drama, the better."

Trever looked at Bella, a bit offended that she interpreted his plans as drama, but realized that she was actually intending to be supportive. There were some things about the Davies family that you just had to get used to.

They gathered around the tree, each with a chosen dessert, or multiple desserts, and beverage of choice. Marco distributed the gifts, one by one.

"Hey Marco! My bedtime is in two hours. You think you can get all those presents in the right hands by then?"

"Oh, Grandpa. If there aren't too many for me, yeah, I can do it." The group laughed at Marco's budding sense of humor. He wasn't born into this family, but he surely did fit in.

Gift after gift, person after person, there were ooo's and ahh's over the thoughtful gifts given and received. Angela and Trevor were showered with gifts, one after the other, at the same pace as the others.

"Hey Ange, what did Trevor get you?" Steve had gotten wind of Trevor's plans and wanted to push the agenda.

"Um…I don't think…" Angela was keenly aware that she hadn't opened a gift from Trevor yet, although the others had each received something from him.

Marco had opened an antique John Deere tractor bank from Trevor. "It's a collector's item that used to belong to my grandfather. Hang on to it Marco, it will be worth a lot one day."

"That's so cool, Pastor Trevor. Thank you."

"Hey Marco," Pauline, who had not been clued in on Trevor's plans, was curious about a missing gift. "Did you miss a present under the tree for Ange from Trevor?"

Marco dove under the tree, now empty of gifts, and looked around.

"I don't see…" Marco paused when he heard a collective gasp. He turned to see Trevor standing in front of his Aunt Ange.

Trevor turned and spoke first to everyone in the room. "As many of you know, Angela and I met last summer, right here in Buffalo Ridge, surrounded by the Davies family. What you may not know, is that we have grown very close since that time, through hundreds of hours on FaceTime, texts and a visit when my father passed."

He faced Angela, dropped to one knee, and took her hands

in his. "Angela, you are the one I have waited a lifetime to meet and an eternity to love. I know we have a lot of logistics to work out, but I don't want to wait any longer to let the world know how I feel about you. I love you. Will you be my wife?"

Angela, flushed and sobbing, took Trevor's face in her hands and pulled herself into him, kissing him hard.

"Was that a yes?" Marco shouted.

"Yes! Yes! That was a YES!" Angela shouted back, hugging Trevor with all that she had.

The room erupted in cheers.

THE EVENING WAS SPENT in celebration, exploring gifts and making future plans. Baby excitement was shared, potential names declared.

"Hey Trevor, Angela, when's the wedding?" Chance never danced around a question. He hit it square on.

"I'm hoping sooner rather than later, although we haven't talked about it yet. I think a good time would be…" Trevor started.

"June, at the gazebo on Canyon Lake, by the swans," Angela finished.

Trevor looked at Angela in amazement. "Really? Are you being serious right now?"

"Yes, if that works for you. The babies should be here by then. Bella, get dude ranch coverage because you're my matron of honor." It suddenly was all clear and planned in Angela's mind.

"Of course, love, I wouldn't miss it."

"Oh, Trevor, is it okay if we don't get married in the church?"

"Angela, we can get married whenever and wherever you want to. There are no rules."

ACKNOWLEDGMENTS

Thank you to Linda Zeppa of Intuitive Writing / Creativity, who enriches my writing life and soulful life with her knowledge, talent, skill, energy, and support. To the talented and proficient Angela Pruden Proofreading, thank you for your continuing support through excellent proofreading talent and encouragement. To those who have or do love me and those who refuse to, thank you for all the lessons! Finally, to my parents, siblings, children and grandchildren, thanks for sharing life's journey, the good, the bad and everything in between. These are the stories that feed the imagination.

ABOUT THE AUTHOR

Kim Smart is a storyteller, nurse, attorney, closing in on her PhD, and student of life. *Grace and Grit* is her eighth published novel and the fifth in the *Buffalo Ridge Ranch Series*. Kim's fiction works are inspired by personalities, experiences, and narratives from her life and the lives of friends and family. Kim has been a lifelong writer and today weaves in stories of the characters she meets at home and across the globe. Kim was raised in South Dakota, where *Grace and Grit* is set.

You can learn more at www.kimsmartauthor.com or through the social media links below.

ALSO BY KIM SMART

Buffalo Ridge Ranch Series

Falling for Home

Two for Love

Taking Chances

Dressing Up Stella

Lynx Creek Chronicles Series

When Fireweed Blooms

Stand-Alone Women's Fiction

Tangled Ribbons

Christmas Market Reunion